SPY PUPS: TREASURE QUEST

Andrew Cope

First published in 2009
by Puffin Books,
a division of Penguin Books Ltd
This Large Print edition published by
AudioGO Ltd 2011
by arrangement with
Penguin Books Ltd

ISBN: 978 1405 664745

British Library Cataloguing in Publication Data available

Printed and bound in Great Britain by
CPI Antony Rowe, Chippenham and Eastbourne

For my favourite mother-in-law

CONTENTS

1. Double Trouble

'Don't be sad, Lara,' soothed Ollie, stroking his dog behind the ear. 'You've still got two puppies left and Mum says we can keep them.'

'And the others have gone to brilliant homes,' added Sophie, trying but failing to sound chirpy.

Lara lay with her head on her paws. She knew the children were right but it didn't stop the pain in her heart. *Hopefully time will heal it*, she thought. *It's so difficult when my babies leave home.* She watched Spud and Star play-fighting. *Bags of energy*, she thought. 'Calm down, you two,' she woofed. 'Why don't you play Scrabble or Monopoly or something a bit calmer?' Her two remaining puppies looked at their mum as if she was mad. Chasing each other around the lounge was much more fun.

Lara reflected on the last four months. *It's been a hectic time*, she smiled. *Becoming a mum of seven, instilling some discipline, getting the pups house-trained and teaching them some of the spy-dog basics. Phew! No wonder I'm always exhausted.*

Lara watched as Spud sat on his sister, squeezing the breath out of her.

'Gotcha!' he barked.

'No, you haven't,' she woofed, twisting away and nipping him on the backside. 'Too slow, bro!'

Lara always knew that most of the pups would be adopted. Dad had explained it to her shortly after she found she was

pregnant. And Lara understood—the house just wasn't big enough to keep them all. Her mission was to find good homes. Each time there was an adoption her tummy churned with happiness and sadness. She was delighted with the new owners. Her eldest daughter, Bessie, had gone to a farmer. He had other dogs and Lara knew they were well cared for. Bessie had a good life ahead of her as a working farm dog. *Perfect*, thought the retired spy dog. *One sorted, seven to go!*

Toddy and Mr G had gone as a pair, hand selected by the police as sniffer dogs. Lara approved. *They are both lively boys*, she thought, *so they will get all the action they crave. And maybe do some good for the world too.* Lara reflected on her spy-dog days and shuddered at the thought of all the baddies she'd stopped, especially her arch-enemy, Mr Big. *I sniffed out his evil drugs empire and put him behind bars. Twice! Maybe my boys will do the same*, she hoped.

Lara had a particular soft spot for Britney. She was the youngest—*a whole nineteen minutes younger than Bessie*—and quietest of the litter. *Seen but not heard*, thought Lara. *Definitely not police dog material but very clever and a great companion. Being selected as a guide dog was perfect*, reflected Lara. *She'll be the top of her class and there will be one very lucky owner!*

TinTin was always going to be a handful. He was a rather strange-looking pup. His brothers and sisters were black and white but TinTin was splodged with brown patches. His energy levels were off the scale and his tail never stopped wagging. He was sometimes a little overenthusiastic. His shaggy coat made him the perfect choice to go and work with his granddad, Leo, in Scotland. TinTin had enrolled to be a mountain rescue dog and his mum couldn't be more proud. *A very worthwhile career. And I know his granddad will take good care of him.*

Lara watched her two remaining puppies chasing around the table legs. *Good homes, all of them*, she thought. *And I'm lucky that the Cook family have let me keep these two.*

'Mum, what's for lunch?' asked Spud, taking a break from annoying his sister.

4

Lara sniffed the air. 'Spaghetti hoops
. . . peas,' she woofed, '. . . and sausages.'

'And when's it lunchtime?' yapped her
son. 'I'm starving.'

'You're always starving!' Lara glanced
at the clock. 'Half an hour,' she replied.

'How long's half an hour?' asked Spud.

'Not long,' she barked, rising wearily to
her feet and stretching. 'Just long
enough to work on those times tables
before we eat!'

2. CAT BURGLAR

Lunch was cleared away and it was time for the pups' afternoon snooze. Lara loved living with the Cooks. *It's not all out adventure and excitement like when I was a spy dog*, she thought, *but we've certainly had more than our fair share of scrapes.*

Lara had adopted the Cooks when they'd turned up at the RSPCA. Before then she'd been working as a spy dog for the Secret Service—the name LARA on her tag actually stood for 'Licensed Assault and Rescue Animal'. But one of her spy-dog missions had gone horribly wrong and her orders were clear. *I was to give myself up to the nearest dog rescue shelter and then adopt a family and wait for help. And I couldn't have chosen better*, she smiled, looking around the room at the Cook children. Ollie had Spud on his knee. The puppy was fast asleep, snoring gently, his chubby tummy breathing in and out. Ollie was the youngest of the children and Lara loved his playfulness. Star and Spud adored him too. Lara watched as Star leapt on to Ollie's lap and snuggled down for an afternoon snooze.

Sophie couldn't help but wander over to her brother and stroke the pups. 'They're sooo cute,' she purred. 'And so squidgy!' Sophie was a true animal lover, destined to become a vet. A chinchilla had been top of her Christmas list for

three years running. 'It's a house, not a bloomin' zoo,' was her dad's favourite comment. He always told Sophie she could have a chinchilla if they traded Lara in exchange. He knew there was no way that would ever happen.

Ben was the eldest and therefore the leader. Although Lara was officially the family pet, he regarded her as *his* dog. The pair would spend hours fishing at the canal or playing football in the garden. Star and Spud were a bit young but had begun to practise their headers and volleys. Star could do forty keepie-uppies and Spud had perfected his goal-scoring celebration—a backflip like he'd seen on TV. It was exhausting and they always needed their long afternoon sleeps!

'I think Star will be a good footballer,' Ben told Lara. 'She's got your natural ability.'

Lara looked across at the sleeping Star. She was a tiny puppy with one sticky-up ear just like her mum. She also had the same trademark black and white splodges, including a patch over her eye. She had tiny razor teeth and a very long

8

tongue that sometimes peeped out when she was asleep. *And so clever!*

Lara watched as Spud woke and wandered over to the games console. *Just puppy fat, I'm sure*, she thought, smiling at his low-hanging belly. Spud was bigger than his sister. *Probably because of his liking for custard creams*, thought Lara. A guilty thought passed through her mind. *I wonder where he gets that from!* Spud was a handsome dog, like his father, Potter. Spud had a shiny black coat and a playful puppy face. His ears were a matching pair: floppy, except when he was concentrating or when someone mentioned food. Then he had the biggest ears in the world, pricked and listening for scrapings into his bowl. *Not quite as bright as his sister*, she considered, *although the BrainBox training game is doing him some good.*

Lara was pleased the building work at home had finished. At first she'd been reluctant when the Secret Service had suggested a security upgrade. But Professor Cortex had been very persuasive, arguing that it would allow her to improve the pet neighbourhood watch scheme that she'd set up.

'And now you're a mother,' the professor frowned, 'you have to be extra careful of enemy agents.'

Lara's office was now complete. She pressed the button with her nose and stood in front of the fireplace. *3 . . . 2 . . . 1 . . .,* she counted, and the hearth moved, rotating Lara into her secret office. She sat at the laptop and fixed her spectacles on the end of her nose. Lara took a pencil in her mouth and logged on to her emails. *Nothing particularly exciting,* she thought, although she was pleased to see a message from Professor Cortex confirming tomorrow's visit to Spy School. *Star and Spud will love it,* she thought. *The professor always has oodles of new gadgets and whacky ideas.*

Lara loved the professor. He was a bit grumpy on the outside but a great big softie on the inside. *He was the one who trained me as a spy dog. And who gave me that ridiculous code name, GM451. I am so pleased the family have chosen to call me by my other code name.*

Lara clicked a remote control and various CCTV camera pictures were beamed on to the screen in front of her. She could see most of the neighbourhood from here. The professor's voice replayed in her head. 'You can never be too careful, GM451. You are the cleverest animal in the world. No other animal can understand every human word. Or defuse a bomb. Or play chess, for that matter.' *And he should know*, thought Lara. *He's head of Spy School. And probably the cleverest, maddest scientist in the world.* Lara couldn't quite see where the danger would come from. *After all, this is a quiet road and I'm retired from active spy-dog service*, she thought. *I can't see that any more baddies are going to come looking for me. But this office is cool*, she admitted, spinning herself round on her leather chair. She cast her mind back over the last year. *Not quite the retirement I'd planned. So many adventures!* Lara shuddered as she remembered falling off a space rocket as it took off, and stopping a diamond robbery. *But being a mum definitely changes things. This time I've given up for real. From now on it's the quiet life for me and the pups.*

11

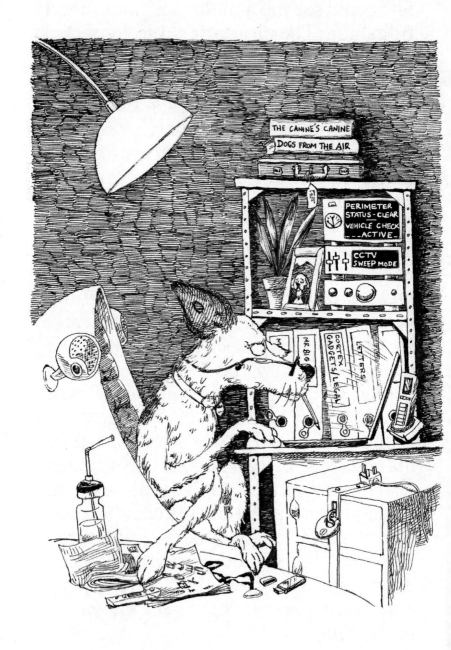

Lara watched on CCTV as Mr Granger from number 42 tipped his grass cuttings into next door's garden. *They won't be happy*, she thought. Through another camera she saw a delivery van pull up at number 7. *New sofa*, she noted. *And what a nice pattern.*

Nothing suspicious, she thought. *No sign of baddies.* Lara zoomed in to the van parked outside number 22. *Window cleaner*, she read. *New bloke, by the look of it.* Lara watched for a minute. The man climbed the ladder and she watched with interest as he looked all around before reaching into the upstairs window and climbing in. *Er, I don't think he should be doing that*, she thought, zooming closer still until she could see through the open window. The CCTV showed the window cleaner snooping around the bedroom, putting trinkets into a bag. Suddenly, Lara was on full alert. She looked at her map of the close. *Number 22, Mr and Mrs Winslow. Both teachers. Both out at work all day! Yikes, I think this is a robbery!*

3. DAYLIGHT ROBBERY

Lara pressed the big red button, adrenalin pumping through her body. She knew the flag would now be raised, alerting her animal neighbourhood watch team to possible danger. Lara had spent months moulding them into a highly responsive unit.

This is their first real test, she wagged. *And a chance for Spud and Star to go through their paces.*

Lara bounded back to the secret door, pressed the button and swung back into the lounge.

'Hi, Lara,' said Sophie. 'Been checking your emails?'

'No time for nice stuff,' barked the family pet. 'Star, wake up! Spud, switch off the BrainBox.' The seriousness of their mum's bark immediately caught the puppies' attention.

'What's up, Ma?' croaked Star. 'Why so serious? I was just resting my eyes!'

'And I was getting my highest score,' complained Spud.

'Robbery,' announced Lara. 'Number twenty-two. Upstairs window. Man with ladder.'

Star and Spud blinked themselves awake and stood to attention. 'We've practised. But this is the real thing. Do you know what to do?' barked their mum.

'Course we do,' yapped Star, sprinting to the garage. 'Plan A. Marbles and nails.'

'That's my girl,' woofed Lara. 'Spud. Are you clear?'

'Yes, ma'am,' barked Spud, raising his paw to his eyebrow in a doggie salute.

'Good, because I'm going to leave you two in charge. This is your first real mission. I've raised the flag so the others will join you. But you two have the lead on this one. Remember, the aim is to capture the baddie but always be safe. I will be nearby if things get hairy.'

'No need, Ma,' replied Spud, turning to chase his sister.

Lara trotted after them, head held high. *Chips off the old block*, she thought proudly.

The burglar crept around the bedroom. He'd done his homework and knew the owners wouldn't be back until late afternoon. Spying a jewellery box he opened it and his eyes lit up with excitement. He took off his backpack and scooped the contents inside.

'Thank you very much for leaving out

all your valuables,' he laughed to himself as he spied a laptop on the desk in the corner.

Worried that the neighbours might notice an empty ladder outside the house, the window cleaner pocketed an expensive-looking watch from the side table and headed towards the window.

* * *

'Quickly, we haven't got much time,' barked Spud out of the side of his mouth, as he carried the bag of supplies. 'He'll be coming down the ladder any minute.'

The puppies sprinted to number 22.

Star took the bag of marbles she'd carried and scattered them at the bottom of the ladder. *And a few along the path*, she thought. *Just for good measure.*

Her brother had taken his bag to the man's van and scattered the contents on the road.

'He's coming,' yapped Star. 'I can see his feet.'

Spud rejoined his sister, and both puppies barked in their wildest voices.

'Remember plan A. Make him panic,' reminded Star. 'That gives us the upper paw.'

The window cleaner came down the ladder as fast as he could. 'Shush, stupid dogs,' he hissed. 'The last thing I need is attention!'

The man's feet hit the ground and he stumbled on the marbles. He began to run but he was going nowhere except downwards. His arms flailed wildly. His feet were a blur before they disappeared from under him and he was left face down on the path.

Spud and Star danced around yapping furiously. They'd slowed him down but now he was angry.

'Pesky dogs,' he growled, spitting out a marble. 'Wait till I get hold of you.' The burglar got cautiously to his feet, rubbing his chin as he did so. He kicked at the marbles. 'Some blasted kids've left their toys lying about,' he cursed, as he tiptoed his way between the glass balls.

'Not so fast, buddy!' barked Spud, grabbing hold of the man's trouser leg and hanging on, ripping the material.

'Shoo, mutt,' snapped the burglar,

kicking out and sending the black puppy flying through the air.

'Leave my brother alone,' yapped Star, jumping at the man and grabbing his bag.

'You can't have that!' yelled the window cleaner, running forward and trying to rugby-tackle the puppy.

But Star was too quick and he rugby-tackled the flower bed instead. Spud, who'd recovered his breath, started to dig like mad, sending mud into the man's face. The burglar wailed as Star jumped on to a nearby wheelie bin and started swaying it towards him. The bin tottered this way and that before eventually falling, its contents burying the burglar. Anger had now turned to fear. The terrified man emerged from under the potato peelings wiping the mud from his face and ran for his life.

Star could hear the burglar's shoes squelching with baked beans and she watched his hands shake as he fumbled for his keys. He opened the door and swung into his van. The engine spluttered into life and he crunched it into gear. He couldn't care less about what he'd stolen, he just had to get away from the evil puppies!

The burglar floored the accelerator and the van lurched forward. There was a hissing sound as the nails that Spud

had scattered around punctured all four tyres, and the pups watched with satisfied smiles as the vehicle came to a halt halfway down the street. Waiting ready for action, dogs and cats emerged from every house to surround the van and George the tortoise arrived on a skateboard. Star and Spud trotted to the scene and congratulated their mum's neighbourhood watch team.

'Nice work, gang,' they woofed, sitting proudly as the police sirens got louder.

The burglar removed a banana skin from his collar and wiped porridge from his face. He was going nowhere. As he opened the door in an attempt to run for it, all the dogs snarled and the cats hissed. Even George tried to look fierce. The man got back into his van and closed the door.

He sighed incredulously as he hit the central locking button. 'I've been nabbed by a pair of puppies.'

4. MINOR MINERS

'Nice work, GM451,' nodded Professor Cortex, holding up the morning paper. *Dogs Foil Cat Burglar*, screamed the headline. 'Did the pups help out?'

Lara nodded while Star and Spud tore around the laboratory re-enacting the capture of the robber.

'First we saw him coming down the ladder,' woofed Star.

'And then we set a trap,' panted Spud.

'Then over he went,' demonstrated Star, tripping and rolling on to her back.

'And *splat*!' whooped Spud, emptying the litter bin over his sister. 'He's covered in gunk. It was so *brilliant*. We want to grow up to be spies like our ma.'

Lara glowed with pride. 'That's all well and good,' she barked, 'but we have to keep our abilities secret.'

'But why, Ma?' asked Spud.

'Because we're family pets,' Lara reminded him. 'Our special intelligence is to be used for emergencies only. Otherwise we'd just bring attention to ourselves and then we'd become some kind of freak show. We'd probably end up on a reality TV programme or something.'

'Cool,' gasped Star.

'*Not* cool,' woofed Lara, raising a warning eyebrow. 'Because we'd also be taken away from the family we love.'

'Whoa! Definitely not cool,' agreed Star.

Professor Cortex had no idea what the dogs were saying. He frowned at the bin-emptying episode. 'Silly names,' observed the head of Spy School. '*Star* and *Spud*. Not very professional, are they, GM451?' he said, peering over the top of his spectacles. 'I think they need code names.'

Star jumped up and down in delight. 'Like proper spies? I could be K9007,' she barked, wagging her whole body. 'The world's first spy puppy!'

'And I'd be GM451 and a half, following in your paw prints, Mum,' wagged Spud.

'No code names, kids,' said Lara. 'You are *not* spies. You are my babies and I don't want you coming to any harm. Or getting into any adventures.' Lara glanced in the mirror and noticed the bullet hole in her upright ear. 'This came from being a spy dog,' she reminded the pups. 'And I've another bullet lodged in my thigh. It's always most embarrassing when I go through airport metal detectors. In fact, I'm very lucky to be alive. I want you guys to grow up as family pets. Spying is just too dangerous.'

The professor noticed the puppies' tails wilt. The old man peered over his spectacles and raised his eyebrows. 'I'm guessing GM451 doesn't want you to have code names,' he said. 'But there's no doubting your intelligence. Check out the screen,' he said, pointing to the large plasma on the wall. 'I have the results of your tests. Kids, come over here,' he shouted to Ben, Sophie and Ollie, who were busy looking at all the strange equipment in the room.

The dogs and the children sat while the professor clicked through some graphs. 'The bar on the left is normal puppy intelligence,' he explained, pointing a chubby finger at the small red bar. 'And here is Agent Spud,' he noted, running his finger to a yellow bar double the size. 'And Agent Star,' he said, beaming at an even bigger bar.

They're not agents, Prof! Lara grumbled but the two pups weren't listening to her.

Star had a huge doggie grin on her face. *Top of the class!*

Spud's shoulders slumped and he dug

an elbow into his sister's ribs. 'Teacher's pet,' he grumbled.

'No, I'm the *children's* pet,' she corrected.

The professor clicked to the next chart. 'Fitness,' he said. 'Average fitness versus the puppy agents. Once again, massive gains,' he noted. Spud sucked his stomach in. 'And strength,' continued the professor. 'Same story.' Spud's shoulders rose as he saw his score go off the chart.

'How's their home training coming on, GM451?'

Pretty good, Prof, nodded Lara.

'They know their times tables,' said Ben. 'And they can understand just about everything we say.'

'My French is coming on,' woofed Star. 'And my brother's specializing in understanding other animal languages. He's quite good at pigeon.' *Although that's because there are only four pigeon words*, thought Star.

'Spud's good at the guitar game on my computer,' offered Ollie. 'And Star is reading *Oliver Twist*.'

'Excellent,' purred the professor. 'It seems the accelerated learning programme is working. Keep up the good work, GM451. I know you don't want your puppies to become spies but it'll do them no harm to learn as much as they can. You never know when special skills may be needed,' he said, tapping the side of his nose. 'Top secret stuff.'

Lara looked at the puppies and felt proud. They were sitting upright, ears to attention, hanging on the professor's every word.

'Speaking of top secret,' continued Professor Cortex, 'I have some new gadgets to show you.'

'Wow!' chirped Ollie. 'This is always my favourite bit of a Spy School visit. The professor has such brilliant gadgets,' he said to the puppies.

'And I've designed some especially for Agents Spud and Star,' smiled the professor, hopping from foot to foot.

'It's happening,' whispered Sophie, nudging her brother. The dogs wagged excitedly and the children began to jump up and down in what Sophie always called the 'mad professor jig'. 'His enthusiasm is catching!'

'I've had a change of job title,'

explained the professor. 'But pretty much the same kind of work.' He smoothed his three strands of hair across his shiny scalp. 'They've moved me into more of a money-making role,' he announced proudly. 'The government is always looking to cut costs so they've reduced the Spy School funding.'

'What do you mean?' asked Sophie.

'Basically, young Sophie, we have to look at new ideas that earn some cash. Inventions that we can sell. It's quite a responsibility,' he nodded, puffing out his chest. 'With the profit ploughed back into research, of course,' he beamed.

Sophie still looked blank.

'Like this,' he said, pointing to a golf club.

'Golf?' stated an unenthusiastic Ben. 'I think you'll find that's already been invented.'

'Quite,' agreed the professor, just about containing his irritation. 'Anyone fancy a swing?' The children followed as Professor Cortex marched outside into the field behind Spy School. He pointed into the distance. 'See that flag over there? That's the hole. What are the odds of Sophie here hitting a hole in one?'

Sophie giggled. 'I've never even held a golf club before,' she said. 'So it must be a million to one shot.'

'Why don't you give it a go?' suggested the professor, handing the golf club to her. 'Like this,' he demonstrated, going through a practice swing.

He rolled a ball at Sophie's feet and everyone stepped back. 'That's right,' she smiled. 'Anything could happen!' Sophie positioned herself near the ball. She'd seen Tiger Woods on the TV and knew roughly how to stand. Her arms swung backwards and she *thwack*ed the ball as far as she could.

'Nice hit,' woofed Spud as the ball looped high into the sky. 'But wrong way. The flag's that way!'

'Whoops,' giggled Sophie as the ball hit the grass. 'Missed by a mile.'

'Not yet,' chuckled the professor, pressing a button on his mobile. 'Keep your eyes on the ball.' Everyone turned back towards the white ball, scuttling across the grass. Mouths fell open as it arced to the left and accelerated along

29

the field—and there was a *plop* as the ball dropped into the hole.

Sophie turned round to the professor, her club raised in the air. 'Hole in one!' she shouted, her eyebrows raised in amazement.

'That's a million to one shot,' agreed the professor. 'I've just shortened the odds a tad. Do you want to know how?'

'Of course,' exclaimed Sophie, joining in with the nodding dogs.

'Simple science,' noted the professor. 'Or should I say, simple genius? Physics. Well, magnetism, to be precise. That's not a normal golf ball, you see. It's a magnet, painted white. And there's a very powerful magnet in the hole. Opposites attract. So long as you hit the ball in the general direction, it's guaranteed to go into the hole.'

'But isn't that cheating?' asked Ben.

The professor stroked his chin, momentarily lost in thought. 'Cheating?' he repeated. 'As in gaining an unfair advantage? Goodness me, no. I like to think of it as using my brain to gain a perfectly fair advantage,' he nodded, reassuring himself with his words.

The gang returned to the lab. 'Any more inventions?' asked Ollie.

'How about these?' suggested the professor, revealing two small helmets. 'They're a bit like miners' helmets with these lights on the front. In fact, I've designed these for Agents Star and Spud.'

'Cool,' wagged Star. 'How do they work?'

'Fix them on to your heads, like this,' said the professor, balancing a helmet on Spud's head. 'Click the strap like so. And, hey presto! A light will show you the way.'

'What's so special about that?' woofed Spud, his tail drooping with disappointment.

'But there's no light,' said Ben.

'You're right, Ben. But this is the clever bit,' enthused Professor Cortex. 'It's environmentally friendly,' he explained. 'You see, we thought, what kind of energy do puppies have?' The professor looked around at the blank faces. 'What do puppies do a lot of?'

'Er, poos?' offered Ollie, thinking of the house-training difficulties of a few weeks earlier.

31

'Yes,' agreed the professor, grinning. 'But what else? How about wagging?' he suggested, his hand waving like a dog's tail. 'You see, the lamps are powered by an infrared sensor that works off the wagging of a tail. The harder the puppies wag, the more powerful the torch! Totally brilliant!'

All eyes fell on Spud's droopy tail. He lifted it and gave a little wag of enthusiasm. The torch glowed. Spud grinned and as he did so his tail picked up speed. The torch beamed with light. 'It works!' he yapped. 'I'm running on wag power!'

Star soon had her helmet strapped on and the pair wagged excitedly around the dark corners of the lab.

'All the best inventions are totally simple,' smiled the scientist. 'And wag power is the simplest concept ever. Just think if all the dogs in the world were wired up, we'd have no need for conventional power stations,' he said, scribbling the idea on a pad.

Everyone agreed it was a great idea. The children left Spy School having been excited by the professor's science lesson yet again. Lara was a little disappointed that she didn't get a wag helmet but she always enjoyed seeing the professor again. She knew he lived for his work and she was proud to have been the first ever graduate of his Spy School.

I think he's proud of me too. But all that spy-dog stuff is history, she thought as they headed home. *My future is here. With my pups and the kids. Spying is for emergencies only!*

5. AN UNEXPECTED BREAK

The kids piled into the kitchen with Lara and the pups, chattering excitedly about the professor's new gadgets.

'Hi, Dad,' said Ben, noticing their father sitting at the table.

Spud and Star bounded round the kitchen, nipping each other and skidding across the floor.

'Hi, kids,' said their dad, sounding distracted.

'Everything OK?' asked Sophie.

'Um, well, it will be but unfortunately your mum's had a bit of an accident this morning. She's fine but she's had to go to hospital.'

'What?' exclaimed Sophie. 'What happened?'

'Oh no,' yapped Lara. 'Kids, calm down,' she woofed, and Star and Spud stopped jumping about.

'Is she going to be OK?' asked Ollie, tears welling up in his eyes.

'Yes, yes, she's going to be fine. She tripped on some stairs and fell down, and, well, she's broken her leg.'

'Poor Mum!' sobbed Sophie.

'Yes, it was very painful for her,' agreed Dad. 'She's going to be on crutches for a while.'

Yikes, thought Lara. She remembered when she broke her leg just before she found out she was having puppies. *It really hurts!*

'How long's she going to be in hospital for?' asked Ollie. 'Who will be doing our tea?' he asked. 'I do like oven chips, Dad, but not every night.'

'They're doing some extra X-rays now,' explained Dad. 'But it's quite a complicated break. Hopefully she'll just be in for a day or two but she won't be able to move around much when she gets home. I've tried to change my working hours but it's difficult. We've decided that it's best if you visit Aunt Aggie while Mum has some rest and gets used to her crutches without the pups under her feet. It's February half-term next week so you can stay a few nights. I spoke to Aggie last night and she said she'd love to have you at her house.'

Ben tried to hide his excitement. He

knew he should be upset for Mum. But Aunt Aggie's house was brilliant—old, rambling and spooky. He nodded wisely. 'I suppose it'd be for the best,' he agreed. 'And we could phone her every day.'

Ollie hadn't learnt Ben's diplomatic skills. 'Aunt Aggie's!' he yelled. 'Spooky Towers. Totally brilliant and fantastic news! Can we go today? Can we go now?'

Ben nudged him. 'Mum's hurt herself, stupid,' he hissed. 'You're supposed to be sad.'

'But Dad says it's not too serious. And Aunt Aggie lives by the sea,' beamed Ollie. 'In that creaky old house. And remember last time we went there, we looked for treasure? The villagers told us of the legend of the lost gold.' Ollie was bouncing up and down with excitement. 'Maybe this time we'll find it.'

'Calm down, Ollie,' soothed Dad. 'It's just a story they made up. But it'd be really helpful if you all agreed to go to Northumberland for half-term. I'll look after Mum and maybe if she feels better soon we can come up north too. I bet the sea air would do her good.'

Even Ben couldn't conceal his excitement now. '*Yesssss!*' he shouted. 'Adventure time. This will be Star and Spud's first time away from home too.' The children grinned at each other before Ben realized they were overdoing the happiness. 'But we'll miss you both, Dad,' he said solemnly.

'And your oven chips,' added Ollie.

'And we hope Mum gets better soon,' nodded Sophie.

And the BrainBox, thought Spud, ears drooped. *No more computer games for a whole week!*

6. SPOOKY TALES

Dad loaded the children and dogs into the people carrier. Lara sat in a seat, strapped in like a human. She fixed her sunglasses in place, plugged her earphones in and switched on her iPod. The pups were banished to a basket in the boot.

Mum was back from the hospital with a big cast on her leg. The kids had kissed and hugged her goodbye and left her surrounded by flowers and magazines to read. Lara had even helped Star and Spud to cover a Get Well card with puppy paw prints.

It was a long car journey but everyone was filled with excitement, especially Ollie. Aunt Aggie lived in the far north of England and to the children it always seemed a remote village miles from anywhere. Dad drove along the coast road and swept past a castle.

'Cor, look at that, everyone,' cooed Ollie.

'That's part of the legend of the gold,' said Sophie. 'We'll get Aunt Aggie to tell us the smugglers' stories tonight. It'll be so exciting to be snuggled up in bed listening to tales of pirates and hidden treasure.'

'Looks like we won't be able to visit the castle, though,' noted Ben. 'That sign says "No public access".'

'And "Trespassers will be persecuted",' said Ollie, pointing to another sign.

'*Prosecuted*,' corrected Sophie. 'And it says "Beware of the dogs". You'll have to be careful, Lara,' she warned. 'Don't want you roughed up.'

Lara took her earphones out and snorted. *I beg your pardon, young lady,*

she thought. *I'm a super-trained secret agent. I'm a karate black belt, if you please. Other dogs need to beware of me!*

The car heaved up the steep hill and stopped outside a large three-storey house. Dad pulled on the handbrake and the children piled out. Ben lifted the tailgate and out sprang Star and Spud, noses immediately to the ground.

Rabbits! So many rabbits! snuffled Spud.

By the time Lara and the pups arrived inside, Aunt Aggie had boiled the kettle and the kids were all sipping hot chocolate.

'Here's Lara,' announced Ben. 'We've told you about her but I think this is the first time you've met her.'

'Pleased to meet you, Lara,' said Aunt Aggie, as Lara rose and offered a paw to shake. 'I've heard such a lot about you. And your adventures! And these two must be Spud and Star,' she said, turning her attention to the puppies. She reached out and scratched behind Star's ear, a satisfied doggie smile spreading across the puppy's face.

The dogs warmed to Aunt Aggie

instantly. She was a homely sort of woman who produced endless cakes and biscuits from the old-fashioned kitchen. The huge stove was always burning away and the air was filled with delicious smells that made Spud's stomach rumble even more than usual. The floor tiles were cracked and loose and the rugs rather threadbare but the house felt lived in.

Plenty of character, thought Lara.

'Lara and the puppies are to sleep in the kitchen. Next to the nice warm oven,' she explained.

The children each had a bedroom of their own. Ben and Sophie had attic rooms with sloping ceilings. Theirs were the coldest rooms because the windows were old and twisted and so they wouldn't shut properly. The February wind was howling around the clifftops, looking for a way in.

'I've got a view of the sea!' yelled Ben, peering out through the grimy glass. 'Looks like there's a storm brewing.'

'And I've got the castle!' yelled his sister from across the landing.

Ollie was to sleep in a large ground-floor room. It smelt musty and there were damp patches of mould on the walls but he didn't care. This was an adventure and he was tingling with excitement. Besides, he had Lara and the puppies sleeping a few doors away.

Dad said his farewells and the children had tried to look sad but failed. They closed the door on the howling gale and went through to the lounge. Aunt Aggie had prepared tea that was wheeled in on a trolley. The TV reception was always so poor that it wasn't worth watching, so Aunt Aggie lit a few candles and put a CD on.

'Tell us the story of the smugglers' gold,' said Ben. 'Lara's a spy dog so you never know, she might be able to solve it.'

Ex-spy dog, reminded Lara with a serious stare. *I'm now a mother of seven. Adventure is the last thing on my mind. I'm too exhausted for a start!*

A distant rumble of thunder rolled across the sky and everyone looked at each other in alarm. 'It's going to be a wild night,' said Aunt Aggie, listening as the wind howled around the chimney pots. 'Exactly as it was two hundred years ago when the gold was shipwrecked.'

Star and Spud gulped and moved closer to their mum.

'Well,' began Aunt Aggie, 'are you sitting comfortably?'

They all nodded, even the dogs. Ollie's eyes were huge with excitement.

'And feeling brave?' Aunt Aggie pulled her cardigan tightly round her and looked up at the children, anticipation shining in her eyes. 'Then I'll begin.'

7. AN ELECTRIC SHOCK

'As you know, this house is called Smugglers' Cottage,' began Aunt Aggie. 'So called because it was famous as a hideout for smugglers and pirates in the eighteenth century.'

Spud and Star cocked their heads to one side, hanging on every word.

Ollie's mouth fell open. 'Like in *Pirates of the Caribbean*?' he asked.

'A bit,' nodded Aunt Aggie. 'Chatterton Castle, which you drove past on the way here, was once owned by a wealthy family who were con artists, crooks and thieves. They worked with the smugglers to lure ships on to the rocks below this house.' Aunt Aggie paused for effect. They could all hear the wind howling and the distant crash of sea on the rocks.

Ollie gulped and Star and Spud huddled even closer.

'Legend has it that many men died on nights like this. The smugglers waved lights from the cliffs and the ships thought it was the signal for safety. But instead their ships were smashed into a thousand pieces.' Aunt Aggie's voice lowered to a whisper. 'There was one particular boat that hit the rocks below. The story goes that it was crewed by pirates who—'

Suddenly, the lights went out and the children nearly jumped out of their skins. Star and Spud ran to Lara, each clutching a leg.

'What's happened to the lights?' asked an alarmed Sophie.

The room was still lit by candles, shadowy flames dancing up the walls. The wind howled and the rain lashed down outside. There was a sudden crack of thunder and Ollie whimpered in alarm.

'Don't worry, Ollie,' reassured Ben, giving his terrified younger brother a hug. 'It's just a power cut, that's all.'

'We've been having plenty of those,' sighed Aunt Aggie. 'This is a lovely place to live but on stormy nights like this we often lose the lights.' She reached for the matches and struck one, curving her hand over it so it wouldn't blow out.

Soon three more candles were flickering away and the room took on an orangey glow.

'Can you finish the story?' asked Ben, the hairs on the back of his neck taut with anticipation. Everyone glanced at Ollie, who nodded bravely.

Aunt Aggie smiled. 'OK, well, where was I? Yes, it was a ship laden with gold. More treasure than you can possibly imagine. On its way to Europe but now stranded on the rocks, with the sea lashing its decks.'

Ollie looked at Aunt Aggie's candlelit shadow. Her head was large and distorted on the wall behind.

'The smugglers couldn't get near the wreck until the storm had died down.' Aunt Aggie lowered her voice again. 'Eventually, when they boarded the shipwreck, it was empty. No crew. No gold,' she whispered. 'No nothing!'

46

The room was silent except for the howling gale and Spud's chattering teeth. A flash of lightning ripped open the sky and illuminated the room.

'So where had the gold gone?' asked Ollie.

'Nobody knows,' said Aunt Aggie mysteriously, thoroughly enjoying telling the story. 'Legend says it was taken through secret tunnels to *this* house and then on to the castle. Nobody survived to tell the tale, yet the gold was gone. Ghost pirates . . .' she said, her voice trailing away. 'The locals told of ghost pirates spiriting the treasure away.'

Another clap of thunder sent Star under her mum's tummy as a draught blew at the candles and they flickered as if to go out.

'And the gold's never been found?' asked Ben.

'Many people have come here looking,' said Aunt Aggie. 'They've even tried to get in and search this house but I've kept them away. The legend says there's a series of tunnels. Maybe the gold's down there somewhere,' she

said, pointing to the ground. 'Under the castle. Or under this very house.'

'Guarded by ghost pirates,' gulped Ollie.

Star's eyes blinked out from underneath Lara.

'*Ghost pirates*,' whined Spud. 'They sound even worse than normal pirates!'

'Don't worry,' assured Lara. 'It's only a story . . .' *At least, I think it is*, she thought to herself.

Another flash of lightning lit the room, closely followed by the rumble of thunder. 'I wouldn't want to be out on the sea tonight,' said Sophie. 'Or living in that draughty old castle.'

'The castle is the key,' said Ben. 'We spoke to one of the locals last time we were here and she said the treasure probably passed through this house but that the castle is the key. That's why they call it the Castle Gold.'

'And we can't get in there,' said Sophie, sounding a little relieved. 'It's closed to the public, isn't it, Aunt Aggie?'

'Yes, that's right. And I doubt you'll be allowed in,' she said. 'It's been bought by an American fellow. Calls himself Lord Somebody or other. He's closed it to the public. In fact, he's pretty unpopular in the local community. Grumpy and horrible. He's even put Rottweilers on guard so no one can sneak in.'

All eyes fell on Lara. She'd encountered a few baddie dogs in her time and usually came out on top, even when she was outnumbered. *No way*, she thought, glaring at her audience. *I'm an ex-spy dog. I don't solve crimes or get into adventures any more. I'm a family pet. End of story.*

'Maybe there's a way,' murmured Ben. 'It's worth looking into.'

Aunt Aggie got up and shuffled off to

the kitchen to find more candles. Little did Lara know that the story was just about to begin!

8. INTRUDER!

Without a TV or computer the children spent the evening playing a board game. Aunt Aggie had a stack of them in the cupboard.

The grandfather clock struck nine and Ollie did one of his famously noisy yawns. 'I see why they call them *bored* games,' he said, stretching his neck and arms.

'Yes, come on, you lot,' said Ben, the yawning spreading like wildfire. 'Early night. Maybe the storm will have blown over tomorrow and we can explore the coast. Maybe even ask Lord Whatsisface if we can visit his castle?'

The children got into their pyjamas and brushed their teeth. Aunt Aggie made three hot-water bottles and each of the children took a candle with them to their bedrooms. Lara settled Star and Spud into the basket by the oven and went to tuck the children in.

She started in the attic rooms where Sophie was tucked up tightly, her eyes peeping from behind the duvet. 'Ghost pirates,' she said. 'I'm sure I can hear them tunnelling, Lara. Listen.'

Lara cocked her head. The gale was howling around the chimney pots and rain was lashing at the windows.

There is a banging sound, she agreed. *A* clunk, clunk, *like someone hammering. Probably just something blowing in the wind*, she thought, planting a doggie lick on the girl's cheek.

She trotted through to Ben, who was just getting into bed. *Night night, mate*, she woofed, allowing him to pat her back. *See you for brekkie. Full English with extra sausages, I hope!* she slurped.

Lara trotted down the stairs to Ollie's room. The hammering sound was louder but Ollie didn't seem to be bothered. The flame on his candle was dancing in the draughty room, eerie shadows licking the walls. 'Night night, Lara,' whispered Ollie.

His pet blew out the candle and licked the youngest Cook child goodnight. *Night night, sleep tight*, she thought. *Don't let the ghost pirates bite!*

*   *   *

Ollie tossed and turned, thoughts of ghostly pirates keeping him awake. He listened to the howling wind and counted the seconds between the lightning and thunder.

Four seconds. That's four miles away, he thought, using the method Ben had taught him. Ollie flicked the light switch near his bed but there was still no power. His curtain was blowing in the draught. All of a sudden there was a scraping at his window, like someone's long nails on a blackboard and Ollie disappeared under his duvet. His heart was thumping.

It's just branches in the wind, he told himself.

Scrape, scrape. There it was again. Ollie peeped out from under his duvet, expecting to see ghost pirates opening the window. He lay still, his eyes peering into the blackness. Then, from the other side of the room he could hear a door squeaking open.

My wardrobe, he panicked. *Do pirates live in wardrobes?* He could just make out the dark wooden door opening. There was the slightest creak and then a soft *thud* as someone's feet landed on the carpet.

Ollie lay frozen with terror. He tried to cry out for Aunt Aggie and Lara but his voice was stuck in his throat. A flash of lightning split the sky and he saw the

black shape of a person walking across the room. Then another flash lit up the room, revealing a man with a huge nose and scary-looking face.

Maybe this is a ghost pirate and he's not real, Ollie hoped. He slid back down beneath the safety of his duvet. *Go away, go away, pirate man*, he repeated to himself, too terrified to speak.

The floor creaked and finally Ollie dared to inch back the duvet just as more lightning brightened the room.

The man was gone.

9. SECRET TUNNEL

Star and Spud came bounding into Ollie's room. Spud jumped on to the bed and Star stood with her paws on the mattress.

'Morning, Ollie,' woofed Spud, burrowing under the duvet to find a face to lick.

A bleary-eyed Ollie surfaced, his hair as wild as last night's storm. He looked around the room. Daylight was creeping in through the window but his room remained dark and gloomy. He could smell bacon. The storm was gone and so was the wardrobe pirate.

'Brekkie time, fella,' woofed Star. 'Everyone's waiting for you, lazybones.'

'Smell that bacon,' swooned Spud.

Ollie swung his legs out of bed and pulled his dressing gown tight. He ventured towards the wardrobe, eyeing it suspiciously. He got halfway and turned back. 'I've got to get my slippers,' he said to the puppies. 'And the floor's cold. Can you open the wardrobe and have a look for me?'

No probs, thought Star, trotting across the room to the large brown wardrobe. Ollie got back in bed and pulled the duvet up to his chin.

Spud joined his sister. It was a big wardrobe and the puppies had to work as a team. Both stood on their hind legs and scratched at the door. Spud levered his paw behind the panel.

'After three,' he woofed. 'One . . .' Ollie pulled the duvet higher. 'Two . . .' he drew his feet up so he was in a ball. 'Three . . .'

The wardrobe door creaked open. Ollie could see dark corners but there was no ghost pirate. Spud and Star took a slipper each and dropped them at the foot of Ollie's bed.

There you go, Your Lordship, thought Spud. *Now can we have our sausages?*

Ollie put his slippers on and walked over to the wardrobe, regarding it warily. He closed the door and turned the key. There was a satisfying click as the door locked and he immediately felt better. 'No more baddies,' he muttered to himself as he followed the two puppies out of the room.

Ollie joined his sister and brother at the table and they chatted noisily to Aunt Aggie.

'You're quiet, Ollie,' noted his aunt. 'Did you sleep OK? Or did the storm keep you awake?'

'Not the storm,' said Ollie. 'Something was scratching at my window and then there was a man in my room.'

Everyone went quiet, except for Spud, slurping his beans.

'*What?*' said Aunt Aggie, alarmed. 'In the cottage? Are you sure, Ollie? I did wonder if that story was a good idea,' she added, turning to look sternly at Ben.

'He came out of my wardrobe,' insisted Ollie. 'He had dark clothes and a big nose.'

Aunt Aggie looked at Sophie and frowned.

'No, he doesn't always make stories up,' said Sophie, reading her aunt's thoughts.

'I'm not making it up,' glared Ollie. 'It really happened. And I was so scared that I hid under my blanket, and when I looked again he was gone.'

'Oh dear. I think I might have overdone the ghost stories,' chirped Aunt Aggie. 'And with the candles and storm—it can make your imagination go wild.'

'My imagination is fine,' declared Ollie. 'I know what I saw.'

Spud finished slurping his beans as Ollie left the table and trudged through to the lounge.

Lara trotted after him. 'There really was a man in my room, Lara,' he told his

59

pet, tearing off a piece of his toast.

I believe you, smiled Lara kindly. *Sometimes dreams can seem very real.* The spy dog decided she'd sleep at the foot of Ollie's bed that night. *Hopefully it'll reassure him*, she thought.

* * *

Lara and the children set off for a walk into the village. Aunt Aggie had given them some money to buy lunch and the plan was to walk along the cliff, towards the castle.

'I'll stay here and bake a cake for afternoon tea,' she smiled. 'You can go and see if Lara can sniff out the treasure!'

Star and Spud were a bit put out at being left behind. Lara had been firm with them. 'You are too young to be out all day,' she woofed. 'Get some rest this morning. Snuggle up in the basket and maybe we'll take you out later.'

'But, Mum,' whined Star, 'staying in is so boring.'

'We want to help find the gold,' complained Spud.

Lara stood her ground. 'We're walking a long way,' she woofed. 'I promise I will take you out this afternoon,' she said, 'providing you prove you can behave for Aunt Aggie. That means no fighting or arguing. And you can practise your numeracy homework, please,' she said, prodding Spud in the chest.

The puppies lay for a while, sulking at the unfairness of it all. 'They get to do all the exciting stuff and we're just supposed to sleep! Or do homework!' grumbled Spud.

'Maybe we can have an adventure all of our own,' woofed his sister. 'Why don't we check out Ollie's story? You know, the tapping on the window. And the man in the wardrobe.'

Spud's eyes lit up. 'Great idea, sis!'

The puppies gambolled into Ollie's bedroom, noses to the carpet.

'There is a strange whiff,' barked Star. 'A sort of musty smell.'

'Probably because the carpet hasn't been vacuumed for years,' laughed Spud.

His sister jumped on to a small table and then on to the window sill. She swished open the curtains, lifting the gloom and blinking at the daylight. The puppy eased the catch with her nose and pushed the window wide open. There was an overgrown bush outside. 'I think I've found his scratching,' she barked. 'The wind blows these branches and they tap on the window. Probably sounds quite scary at night,' she said, dragging her claw down the glass to make a horrible screeching sound.

'Good detective work, sis,' woofed Spud, his nose still twitching at the carpet. 'We'll make a spy dog out of you yet! Hop down and check this out.'

His sister joined him and the two puppies stood by a boot print. 'It's a size ten at least,' said Star. 'It's nearly as big as me! And it smells fresh.'

'Who wears size tens in this house?' asked Spud. The pups looked at each other, their tails wagging excitedly.

'Nobody!' they chorused.

'Maybe Ollie was right?' said Star, sniffing the carpet. 'Here's another muddy print. And another!' she yapped, following the boot prints to the wardrobe. Star gulped. She scratched at the wardrobe door. 'It's locked,' she woofed, looking up at the key.

Spud went over to the chair and pushed it towards the wardrobe. 'Let's check it out,' he woofed. 'We need to turn that key.'

The dogs scrambled on to the chair but still couldn't reach the key.

'Shoulders,' said Spud. 'You stand on my shoulders and we're there.' He bent down and his sister scrambled up. 'Ready?' he asked.

'When you are,' she replied, and her brother heaved up on to his hind legs, raising his sister to key level. She fumbled for a minute—it was difficult with paws instead of hands!

63

Eventually the key turned and Spud was glad to put her down. They dragged the chair away and Star put her paw into the crack of the opening and pulled.

'Here goes,' she said as the hinges creaked open. Inside it was empty apart from some old coat hangers.

'Nothing! Phew!' said Spud.

Star jumped into the wardrobe and sniffed hard. 'Woodworm. Moths,' she decided. 'But, hmmm, that's the whiff of a person! And not someone I recognize.'

'Yikes,' barked Spud. 'Why would a stranger have been hiding in Ollie's wardrobe?'

'No idea, Sherlock,' said Star. 'But smell this,' she said, snuffling at the back of the wardrobe.

Spud scrambled inside to join his sister. 'Fresh air,' he said. 'There must be a hole at the back.' Spud sat down, his bottom hitting a small lever. 'Whoa!' he barked.

The back of the wardrobe slid away to reveal a black hole.

'No way!' yapped Spud, looking wide-eyed at his sister. 'A secret tunnel!'

'A smugglers' passageway,' wagged his sister. 'And a chance to explore!'

'You're not serious,' protested Spud. 'We're not going down that spooky tunnel, are we?'

Too late. His sister had already bounded to the kitchen and dragged the professor's kitbag back to the bedroom. She picked out her torch hat. 'Come on!'

'Are you sure, sis?' questioned Spud. 'Mum said we could go out later if we behaved.'

'Well, we can go out now, silly,' woofed Star. 'And we're not misbehaving, we're being trainee spies. Mum would do exactly the same. Let's follow this tunnel and sniff out whoever's been sneaking around Ollie's room.'

Spud thought carefully about what trouble they would be in if their mum found out. *What if we're not around for Aunt Aggie's cake and our walk this afternoon?* But the idea of finding treasure was just too tempting. Anyway, they could just take a look inside the tunnel and their mum would never even have to know.

'OK!' he yapped.

'Good,' said Star. 'Now stop worrying and help me with this.'

Spud pulled Star's torch hat on straight, then used his teeth to snap the clasp in place. Star returned the favour and the dogs looked at each other, their headlamps shining brightly as their tails wagged with excitement.

'Let's do it,' commanded Star. 'Let's have our first ever spy-pup adventure!'

10. GOLD DIGGER

It was a breezy day but the rain from last night's storm was gone. Lara bounded ahead of the children.

So many rabbits, she thought, nose to the ground. *It's doggie paradise!*

They followed the narrow road from Aunt Aggie's towards the sea.

'Wow!' exclaimed Ben, gazing out over the cliffs. 'Look at the jagged rocks down there,' he said. 'It's no wonder there were so many shipwrecks.'

The group strode along the path towards the castle. It was a magnificent building that stood high on the cliff, looking out to sea. Half was in ruins but the other half had been rebuilt, the turrets rising royally over the town below. An American Stars and Stripes flag billowed from the flagpole.

Lara bounded ahead. *It sure is an impressive building*, she thought, looking up at the sturdy walls.

The children joined her, and Ben had to shout to make himself heard above the wind. 'Let's see if we can get in,' he yelled.

They approached the huge wooden door. It was five times taller than Ben and had a rope hanging at its side. Ben hesitated for a moment before pulling it.

'Cool doorbell,' cooed Ollie.

They waited for a minute. 'Nothing,' said Sophie, sounding rather relieved.

Lara cocked her head and listened. *No, nothing*, she agreed. *Nobody home.*

The children turned to go as two men approached from the village. One was a policeman in a dark blue uniform. The other was speaking very loudly in an American accent. Sophie winced at his clothing choice of bright pink trousers and lime green jumper.

'What are you kids doing up here?' yelled the American as he came towards them. 'Can't you see it's private?'

'His voice is as loud as his clothes,' whispered Sophie.

'Er, we did see the signs,' admitted Ben, 'but we thought it was worth asking. Our aunt says there's old treasure hidden in this area and we just wanted to have a look around, if that's OK?'

As the two men stalked up to the children, Ollie jumped as he recognized the policeman. His big nose was unmistakable—it was the man from his bedroom the night before, he was sure! He shrank behind his brother.

'Well, it sure ain't OK,' bellowed the man, glaring at the children. 'And keep your pesky mutt away from my castle. I don't want dog doos everywhere.'

Me neither, thought Lara, taking an instant dislike to the man. *I'm toilet-trained, if you please. And I'm neither pesky nor a mutt. I'm actually a highly skilled spy dog.*

'Do you own the castle?' asked Sophie.

'Gee, ain't she the bright one,' the man

yelled. 'Do I sound like a local?' he asked. 'I ain't from these parts, little lady. My name's Art Burlington. From New York City. I'm also lord of this castle. My friends call me "Art" so you can call me "Lord Burlington".' He gave the children a smug look and Lara couldn't help but raise her hackles. 'I bought the castle as, let's say, an investment.'

'For the gold?' asked Ben.

'What do you think, sonny?' shouted the lord, his face as pink as his trousers. 'I sure didn't buy it cos I wanted to live here. Awful place and awful weather,' he added, staring out to sea.

The policeman eyed the children suspiciously. 'You lot aren't from round here, are you?' he enquired. 'Not seen you before.'

'No,' began Sophie. 'We're staying with our aunt. At Smugglers' Cottage.'

Both men stiffened. They exchanged glances and then looked back at the children. 'Smugglers' Cottage, eh?' repeated Lord Burlington. 'It's a draughty old cottage, ain't that right, PC Winkle? Awful place. Power cuts, if I'm not mistaken. Well, your Aunt Agatha has been very difficult,' he said, glancing at the policeman. 'What your aunt probably hasn't told you is that I've offered to buy her rundown cottage. In fact I've made several offers. Very good offers. But the stubborn old lady won't budge.'

'Aunt Aggie isn't a stubborn old lady,' said Ben defensively. 'That cottage is her home. What do you want to buy it for anyway?' he asked suspiciously.

'None of your business,' snapped PC Winkle.

'Is it the gold?' questioned Ollie, stepping out from behind Ben. 'I-I-I saw you snooping round my room last night,' he said bravely, pointing to the policeman. 'Were you looking for the gold?'

Lord Burlington boomed with laughter.

'Ollie!' said Sophie. 'You can't accuse a policeman of that!'

'Never you mind why His Lordship wants to buy the cottage,' PC Winkle snarled as Ollie retreated behind Ben's back again. 'And I wasn't snooping in your bedroom. Listen to your sister—that's a ridiculous thing to say to a policeman,' he stuttered, turning bright red with rage. 'Now you lot run along and take this flea-ridden mutt with you.' Lara had to dodge his huge boot as he aimed it as her.

Er, excuse me, thought Lara. *I'm a karate black belt—you don't want to take me on. And I pride myself on cleanliness. I have a shower every morning. I even use Ben's shower gel. There are no fleas on me, matey.*

'You need to remind your stubborn

Aunt Agatha that we've made our best offer,' added the lord. 'She needs to sell up and move out before the power cuts become even more regular. Don't you agree, PC Winkle?' he smirked.

'Yes, Lord Burlington, that's right. And please don't come round here again. Not only is it private property but it's dangerous, see,' added the policeman. 'We wouldn't want anything nasty to happen now, would we? Like your dog getting hurt, for instance.'

Lara growled at the men. *Just try it*, she dared.

'Don't worry, we won't be coming back here,' said Sophie as she turned to leave.

Ben dragged Lara away and the children headed down the hill.

Lara was angered by the men's unfriendly attitude. *I'm tempted to do some martial arts on those two*, she thought, *but I'm only supposed to do it in self-defence. And fleas? How dare he!*

'Scary,' said Ben.

'Yes,' agreed his little brother. 'Pink trousers. More like terrifying!'

'Not his clothes, silly. His attitude.'

A yellow digger chugged up the track

73

and they watched as the gate opened and it pulled into the castle grounds.

'I bet he's digging for gold,' said Ben. 'He's bought the castle on the cheap, closed it down and is now ripping it apart. It'd be awful if a horrible bloke like that actually found the treasure.'

It'd be criminal, thought Lara.

'What did you mean about PC Winkle being in your room, Ollie?' asked Sophie. 'You're not serious, are you? Aunt Aggie's story just put silly ideas in your head.'

'It was *definitely* him,' blurted Ollie. 'The policeman. I didn't imagine it, I promise. I saw his face in the light from the storm—his nose was exactly the same.'

'The policeman was in your room?' repeated Sophie.

'He came out of my wardrobe,' said Ollie. 'He really, *really* did.'

'OK, Ollie, we believe you,' said Ben, squeezing his younger brother's shoulder.

The older children were puzzled. It was unusual for Ollie to tell lies and they knew by his voice that he really believed what he was saying.

Lara slunk along, head down, thinking hard. *OK, so I'm retired from spying*, she thought. *But castles, hidden gold, a smugglers' cottage and policemen in a wardrobe. This is going to need some investigating!*

11. CAPTURED!

'You first,' said Spud, pushing his sister from behind. 'It was your idea.'

Star took a deep breath and entered the tunnel, her wag-powered torch lighting the brickwork on the walls. Spud followed, providing extra light. It was a decent-sized opening, high enough for a child Ollie's age to stand upright. But an adult would have to bend double.

The puppies ventured onwards, following a series of stone steps that dropped deeper in the direction of the cliffs. The steps stopped as the tunnel flattened out, and Star and Spud stood with their lights shining into the eerie distance. There were a few cobwebs and the sound of dripping water, but apart from that, nothing.

'Come on,' urged Star, her bark echoing into the distance. 'Let's see if we can sniff out an adventure!'

The dogs followed their noses, scampering into the darkness. They came to a fork in the tunnel and decided to investigate the left-hand side first.

'Whoa, some steep steps,' barked Star, the light picking out a downward path carved into the rock. Within a minute they saw daylight and scampered out of a cave on to a pebble beach.

'Wow!' woofed Spud, looking around at the steep cliffs. 'This looks like the only way on to this beach. I bet this is where the pirates collected the shipwrecked treasure and hauled it through the tunnel. To Smugglers' Cottage!'

The puppies sat and rested a while, their lights glinting in the gloomy weather. Waves crashed against the

77

rocks and thousands of pebbles churned around in the powerful ocean before crashing on to the beach.

'There's no way that ships would survive on these rocks,' woofed Star. 'Easy pickings for smugglers.'

The pups re-entered the cave and headed back to the fork in the tunnel. 'Right takes us home,' said Star.

'So left it is,' woofed Spud, getting a taste for adventure. 'You're right, this sure beats sitting around the house. And it's a hundred per cent better than homework!'

The dogs scampered along the tunnel until they eventually came to a metal grille. 'It's locked,' said Spud, 'but I reckon we might be able to squeeze through the holes.'

'Good idea,' said his sister. 'Let's give it a go.'

Star breathed in and she was through. Spud stuck his head through but was soon regretting his extra bacon butty. Whichever way he tried, his tummy got stuck. Eventually, he stood on his hind legs, breathed in as deeply as he could and squeezed his hardest. Star pulled and her brother popped through the gap like a cork.

'Made it!' yelped Spud, looking at the scratch marks on his side. *No second helpings from now on! And no finishing Star's leftovers!* 'Where are we?' he asked, looking around at the stone walls.

'Not sure,' shrugged his sister. 'But I suspect we might be in the castle.'

A shiver went up Spud's spine. 'What if there are baddies? Or ghost pirates?'

Star's eyes shone with excitement. 'Well, let's see what we can find, then go home and tell Mum. She's a spy dog. She'll know what to do.'

The puppies looked around and decided they were in the castle dungeon.

'Good job we've got Professor Cortex's torches,' said Spud. 'Otherwise it'd be totally scary.' His woof echoed through the big empty space and the puppies made sure they stayed close together. They sniffed for a way out.

'There are more steps over here,' said Star, tiptoeing up them. The winding staircase ended in a heavy wooden door that was wedged open with a box of apples. They climbed over the crate and jumped down into a room that looked like the castle kitchen.

'Light at last,' said Spud, stopping his wagging to dim the light.

'Careful,' hissed Star. 'I can hear footsteps.'

The pups shrank into a nearby corner with their tails drooped as a burly lady hurried by. She was carrying a pile of plates and the pups heard them crashing into the sink as she began the washing-up.

Spud could smell food. *Lots of lovely food*, he thought. *Roast beef. And spuds. Oooh, and gravy. I love gravy*, he thought, his mouth watering.

Star nudged her brother. 'Stop slobbering. We're not here to eat. And we'll need to squeeze back through those bars,' she warned. 'We're here to find information that can solve this mystery.'

But Spud couldn't concentrate. He could hear the cook scraping leftovers into the bin. He loved the sound of scraping plates because it always meant there would be something exciting in his doggie bowl. *I wonder if they've got any Yorkshire puds left over*, he wondered, creeping out of the shadows.

'Spud,' whined his sister, 'get back here!'

Spud's ears had stopped working like they always did when he was hungry. *Roast beef*, he thought, following his nose towards the bin. He saw a huge slice of lemon meringue pie on the table. *And pudding too! Oh boy!* His tail was on autopilot—his torch shining brightly.

Star sneaked out from her hiding place and grabbed his tail with her teeth in an

attempt to pull him back. But Spud was bigger and stronger than his sister and she was dragged out into the middle of the castle kitchen.

If the cook turns round, we're doomed. Star let go of her brother and scurried under the table. She watched in agony as he sniffed his way to the bin.

He licked at a few gravy puddles and then sat there wagging his tail, looking up at the cook. *Any roast beef?* he thought, his torch shining on the back of the lady's head.

The cook had her hands in the soapy water. She reached for another batch of dirty plates and turned to scrape the leftovers into the bin. As her foot hit the pedal she stopped in amazement, blinking hard at the puppy.

'A dog!' she exclaimed. 'A tiny dog? With a miner's helmet!' The cook dried her hands and bent down, grabbing Spud by the collar. 'What on earth are you doing in my kitchen?'

12. KITCHEN CHAOS

Star expected the worst. Maybe for her brother to be taken outside and sent away, leaving her alone in the kitchen. But to her surprise the lady cradled Spud and stroked him lovingly.

'I love dogs,' she cooed. 'And you are so cute. And that's a lovely hat. What's your name, little fella?' she asked.

'Er, Spud,' woofed Spud, fixing his best doggie grin.

The lady checked his collar. 'Well, how do you do, Spud,' she smiled. 'Know what?' she grinned. 'Dogs aren't allowed in my kitchen. You'll be in big trouble if they catch you.'

Well, I could just have some secret roast beef and be on my way, wagged the puppy.

'So let me lock you in here for the afternoon. And then you can come home with me later.'

Star's eyes bulged with horror as her brother was carried to the pantry. 'Let's get you some dinner,' she said. 'And then you can have a snooze.'

Dinner, thought Spud. *You mean pie? Brilliant idea. And a snooze. Perfect!*

The cook turned towards the plates stacked up near the sink.

Star groaned. *That's why he can't squeeze through tight gaps*, she thought. *Run for it, bro! While her back's turned. Quick!*

But Spud just sat and wagged as the lady scraped some food into a saucer and placed it on the floor. His eyes beamed as brightly as his torch.

'See you later, Spud,' she said, closing the door on the puppy. 'You're my little secret, don't you worry.'

Star smacked her paw to her forehead. *No way!* she thought. *Now the Roast Beef Kid's got himself trapped!*

She stayed hidden while the kitchen staff hurried about their business.

'Get that apple crumble ready, please!' shouted the cook, who had hidden Spud.

A man shuffled past Star as she shrank back into the corner. But she realized too late as he bent down to pick up the crate of apples that was holding the dungeon door open.

Stop it, buddy! That's our way out! But

there was nothing she could do as the man picked up the box and let the door slam closed behind him. *Spud, your stomach's got us in real trouble now*, she panicked, trying to think of another way out of the kitchen. She checked for other exits. *All shut. How many people do we have to get past?* she wondered, counting the staff. *Two cooks, one helper*, she spied, *and a butler.* She noticed the second cook put hot food into a small cupboard, then press a button and it disappeared. *I think that's called a 'dumb waiter'*, she remembered from her history homework. *The food is hauled upwards in a kind of lift until it reaches the dining hall. Then there's a waiter at the other end who serves it to the guests. The dumb waiter is probably our best way out.*

The puppy sat carefully watching the pattern of work in the kitchen, waiting for a chance to free Spud and escape. She crept from under the table and dodged a few clumsy feet. *Careful not to wag*, she thought. *Or the light will give me away.* The puppy tiptoed closer to the larder door. *Still closed.* She cocked her head and pricked her ears to their full height. Her brother was slurping away inside. *Totally ruled by his stomach*, she tutted.

Star watched for a moment and leapt up on to the draining board. She jumped into a big saucepan that had been washed. *Good job I'm small*, she thought, peering over the top of the pan. Star remembered one of the rules of spying that her mum had taught her. *Chaos*, she thought. *Create chaos and then keep your head when all around are losing theirs.* She waited for the right moment.

The kitchen assistant picked up the pan, tea towel in hand. Star popped her head out of the pan and barked her loudest bark. *Boo!* she thought, putting her paws in her ears and sticking her tongue out at the woman. There was a scream and the pan went into the air. Star jumped for her life and the pan hit the tiled floor with a clatter.

'A dog!' yelled the lady. 'There's a dog in the pan.'

The cook came over to see. 'What do you mean "a dog"?' she asked, thinking of Spud locked safely in the pantry. 'A puppy!' yelled the woman. 'A horrible rat of a dog. With a silly hat on!'

86

The cook looked alarmed. She knew about a puppy with a hat on, but she'd locked it in the pantry. She went to the pantry door and opened it to peep inside, imagining Spud might have escaped.

Star jumped on to a kitchen shelf, dislodging as many pots and pans as she could. The noise was deafening. She did a flying leap at a huge bag of flour, which split open and the contents puffed out and filled the kitchen like a snowstorm.

Star barked at the top of her voice. 'Come on, Spud!' she yelled. 'This is a distraction and the door's open. Run for it!'

Spud's tummy was finally full so his ears were working again. *That's Star! Oops, better get a move on!* He looked at the crack in the doorway and went for it.

'Hey, Spud, come back here!' shouted the cook as he dived between her legs.

The other kitchen staff were in a mad panic, arms flapping wildly. The cloud of flour made it difficult to see but Spud wagged hard, his torch picking a way through the floury fog. The butler came at him with a broom, which the puppy dodged as he raced in the direction of his sister's yapping.

Star swept her paw across the shelf, firing a couple of eggs towards the butler. *Direct hit!* Then she jumped off the shelf on to the scales, sending a lump of butter high into the air. *Splat! Gotcha!* she thought, landing a hit on the cook.

The butler skidded on the broken eggs and trod in a saucepan, his heavy foot clanging towards the puppies.

'Follow me, bro!' yelled Star, bounding on to the table and heading for the small lift. Spud's heavy tummy was slowing him down.

The flour fog was clearing and the butler's broom crashed down again, millimetres from his head. It gave him the extra surge of adrenalin to leap towards the dumb-waiter lift.

Star hit the button and slammed the door shut. 'Bye bye, everyone!' she barked as the puppies were hauled upwards into the castle.

13. CASTLE INN

The Cook children wandered into the village, their heads spinning after the encounter outside the castle.

'Let's grab a drink and a snack while we figure things out,' suggested Ben, pointing to the Smugglers' Cafe across the road. 'Look,' he smiled, 'it's got a sign saying dogs are welcome. Perhaps we can get Lara a hot drink too.'

And a cake, she thought, wagging hard. *Then I'd better get back and check on the pups. I don't want them causing any mischief for Aunt Aggie.*

The children and Lara sat down and peered at the menu. The waiter arrived and Ben ordered four hot chocolates. The man looked surprised. 'But there are only three of you,' he said.

Lara wagged hard and winked at the man. *Think again*, she panted. *I'm not missing out.*

'Um, I really like chocolate,' said Sophie, giving him her sweetest smile.

The children looked around at the cafe

as they waited. There were all sorts of ancient pictures on the walls. 'Lots of paintings of ships,' pointed Sophie. 'On the high seas. I bet one of those is the galleon that had the gold.'

'And portraits like in haunted houses,' noted Ollie. 'They might be the smugglers and pirates.'

'And check out that suit of armour,' said Sophie. 'You'd hardly be able to walk if you wore that!'

Four hot chocolates arrived and the waiter chatted to the children. 'On your holidays?' he asked cheerily.

'Yes,' said Ben. 'We're staying at Smugglers' Cottage with our Aunt Aggie.'

The man smiled. 'I know your aunt. A bit spooky up there, I bet,' he said. 'Have you heard the tales?'

'Of the gold?' asked Ollie. 'Yes, we think the man in the castle's digging it up.'

The cafe owner laughed. 'Many have searched,' he said, 'but nobody's ever come close. They reckon there are tunnels carved below the town. Ancient walkways where the smugglers stashed their loot. Quite a network down there, I reckon.'

'And what was this place in the old days?' asked Ben looking around the room.

'Oh, this cafe has been in my family for generations,' said the man. 'My wife and I took it over five years ago and have brightened it up a bit. And given it a more exciting name. Smugglers' Cafe sounds better than the old name.'

'What was it called before you took it over?' asked Sophie.

'The "Castle Inn",' nodded the man. 'We thought it was a bit boring. It's the oldest building in town, almost as old as the castle itself. This inn was where the smugglers and pirates used to come for a drink and a room for the night. Check out that armour,' he said, pointing to the fireplace. 'That's been here forever. A relic from olden times. Too heavy to move!'

The owner wandered off to serve some other customers and Ollie quickly put the last hot chocolate on the floor beside Lara.

The castle, thought the spy dog,

slurping the whipped cream from the top of her drink. *Where smugglers and pirates used to hang out. Hmmm.*

Ben picked the marshmallows from his mug, his eyebrows almost meeting in the middle. 'The "Castle Inn" . . . I wonder . . . Lara, are you thinking what I'm thinking?'

I think so, buddy, nodded Lara, lapping up the sweet drink.

'Thinking what?' asked Sophie.

'For the last hundred years people have been searching for gold,' said Ben, looking around at the relics on the wall.

'Yes,' nodded Sophie. 'In the castle.'

Ben swept his hand around the room. 'What if, for all these years,' suggested her brother, 'everyone's been looking in the wrong castle?'

14. VIEW FROM THE TOP

The dumb-waiter lift stopped and Star and Spud popped the door open. They both peered out of the hole in the wall.

'Wow!' gasped Spud. 'It's huge!' They had ended up in the main castle dining suite, where two men were seated at the longest table they'd ever seen. One was dressed like a policeman and the other had bright pink trousers and was shouting in an American accent.

'I can't wait any longer!' he yelled. 'We've done just about as much digging as we can and there's nothing. Not a single gold coin. Not even a brass farthing! The gold's not here, PC Winkle. I think it must be hidden in Smugglers' Cottage.'

Star and Spud jumped silently from the lift and hid behind a vase. Their ears pricked. 'That's Aunt Aggie's cottage,' murmured Spud.

'Well, the lady won't sell to us,' replied PC Winkle. 'We've even cut off the electricity to make life uncomfortable but she won't budge. There's not much more we can do, Lord Burlington.'

'There's always more!' bellowed the lord. 'I've ploughed everything into this castle. My personal fortune has gone. I need to find that gold.' There was a munching sound as he shovelled some lemon meringue pie into his mouth. 'I *have* to find that gold!' he drawled, spitting pastry on to the table.

'Well the investigation hasn't been a complete waste,' offered the policeman. 'We found the tunnel. Shall I go down it again tonight, boss?' More pie was shovelled. 'It's a bit difficult because she's got those horrid brats staying. But I can creep around and see what I can find.'

'No point messing about,' shouted Lord Burlington, wiping his mouth with a napkin. 'It's too slow.'

'What shall we do, then?' asked PC Winkle.

'You're a copper, ain't you? You'll have

to take the law into your own hands,' smirked the American. 'Maybe Agatha knows more than she's letting on. Let's pay her a visit and see if she'll talk.'

The policeman looked unsure. 'What do you mean?' he asked hesitantly.

'What do you think I mean, you idiot?' snarled the lord. 'I've got everything resting on this treasure.' He stood up and marched towards the vase. Star and Spud shrank as small as they could. The man went over to a glass display box and pulled out an ancient flint pistol. 'Maybe this will jog her memory,' he glared.

'That's a bit, er, d-d-drastic, Your Lordship,' stuttered PC Winkle.

'There're millions at stake,' barked the American. 'Gee whizz, man, you're one of the boys in blue. You're supposed to be brave.' Lord Burlington examined the gun and cocked the trigger with a satisfying *click*. He waved it at the policeman. 'Are you in?'

PC Winkle looked down the barrel of the ancient weapon and gulped. 'Most definitely in,' he mumbled.

'OK,' said the lord. 'Let's go and pay Agatha a visit.'

Spud was open-mouthed in horror. *Yikes*, he thought, tapping his sister on the shoulder. *He's got a gun*, he pointed. Spud peered back out from behind the vase and accidentally caught it with his large behind. The vase wobbled. The puppies looked up and Spud let out a woof of alarm.

'Whoops,' he yapped. 'That was clumsy of me.' The vase wobbled dangerously. *I hope it's not expensive*, he thought as the priceless pot crashed to the ground.

The policeman jumped to his feet in alarm. 'What's that?'

'That's my antique vase!' bellowed Lord Burlington.

'Spud! You've done it again,' hissed Star, the puppies now on display.

Maybe I can fix it? offered Spud, looking at the thousands of pieces of china scattered across the floor. *Then again, maybe not!*

'Dogs!' yelled the lord. 'How did they get in here?'

At that moment the butler burst into the room, covered in eggs and flour. 'Sorry, Your Lordship,' he stammered, 'but have you seen some dogs? With helmets. There's chaos in the kitchen.'

PC Winkle pointed at the puppies, cowering in the corner.

Hi, smiled Spud, his torch shining in the butler's eyes. *Thanks for the dinner. But I think we'd better be going now.*

'Get them!' yelled the American. 'I'll release the guard dogs,' he shouted, hitting an alarm button on the wall. 'That'll be the end of them.'

Star looked at Spud. *'Yikes!'* she yelped. 'Guard dogs! Mum warned us about them.'

'What did he mean *that'll be the end of us*?' gulped her brother.

'Let's not wait to find out,' she yapped. 'We need an escape plan. And fast!' Star scanned the room looking for the best exit.

The butler tried the softly softly approach, tempting the puppies with some roast beef. Luckily, Spud's tummy was full so he resisted. Star darted for the door but PC Winkle had jumped up to guard it. He reached for one of the swords hanging on the wall and held it in both hands. 'Diced puppy,' he snarled, swishing the blade at Star.

Her little legs turned and ran, her tail tucked in, protecting it from the chop.

Spud was working on a plan of his own. He leapt at the huge curtain and hung on with his teeth. He growled through the side of his mouth. 'Come on, come on,' he urged. He heard a tear and the huge drapes fell to the floor, snaring the butler in a velvet trap. 'Curtains for you!' woofed Spud, pleased with his handiwork. 'One down, two to go.'

PC Winkle was waving the sword dangerously.

'Careful with that thing!' yelled Lord Burlington, jumping out of the way. 'Come here, puppies. I have something for you.'

Yes, thought Spud, *something horrible.* The little dog backed away from the man, snarling as viciously as he could. 'And I've got something for you! See these teeth?' he growled. 'They're going to end up in your bottom if you're not careful. My mum's a spy dog, you know!'

The lord crept forward, arms out wide, trapping the dog into a corner.

'Get away from my brother!' yelled Star, leaping at the man and sinking her teeth into his pink trousers. 'You're a baddie and I hate baddies,' she snarled, hanging on to the man's backside for dear life.

Lord Burlington flapped at the dog. 'Get off my butt, mutt!' he yelled.

PC Winkle swung his sword and another priceless vase hit the floor. He lashed out at Spud and the sword ripped through an oil painting.

Behind them all the heavy wooden door creaked open and there stood two snarling Rottweilers. They were straining at their leashes, choking themselves in their enthusiasm to enter the mayhem.

The head of security pointed to Star and Spud. 'There they are, fellas,' he said. 'Kill!'

'Kill?' yapped Spud. 'Don't much like the sound of that!'

Star gulped. 'What are we going to do?'

The security guard fiddled with the dogs' collars and the huge black animals catapulted from their leads.

15. DOGS ON A WIRE

Heads down, the Rottweilers pelted across the dining room, their claws hammering on the tiles. Star and Spud had no time to think.

'Follow me!' yelled Star, her tiny puppy legs sprinting for the stairs.

Spud was slower, his heavy tummy acting like a handbrake. Up the stone stairs they went. Round and round, up the castle turret.

'These steps go on forever,' barked Star.

She could hear her brother panting behind her. She could also hear heavy paws galloping up the stairs. The Rottweilers were in hot pursuit, their long legs bounding effortlessly upwards.

Star burst out at the top of the tower. *It's a shame there's no time to look at the view*, she thought. *I bet you can see the whole town from here.*

Spud joined his sister, his tongue lolling out of his mouth. 'Too ... many ... stairs!'

Together they slammed the door. 'Get that stone,' said Star, 'and stick it under the door. It'll buy us some time, like Mum taught us.'

Spud nosed the stone towards his sister and they shoved it under the door just as the Rottweilers arrived. They hurled themselves at the door, barking and scratching furiously.

'It won't hold them for long,' she woofed. 'We need a way out. And quick!'

'Check the view,' said Spud. 'You can see for miles! And look down there,' he pointed. 'All those yellow diggers in the castle grounds. What a mess!'

Star had a quick look. 'I guess that's the lord digging for treasure,' she woofed. 'But we haven't got time to admire the scenery!'

'Hey, there's Mum and the kids,' waved Spud. 'I wonder if they can see us. Hi, guys!'

Star tutted with frustration. Her brother could be so stupid sometimes. *Doesn't he realize the seriousness of the situation?* 'We have to find a way out of this mess and get a message to Mum. Aunt Aggie could be in trouble. That baddie has a gun, remember?'

'And those dogs have sharp teeth,' wailed Spud, listening to the angry barks behind the door. 'We're doomed!'

'We're never doomed,' declared his sister. 'Mum always says to think of a spy-dog solution. So think, bro, think.'

Spud walked around the tower. It was a sheer drop every way he looked. He spied the flagpole. 'What about that?' he pointed.

'What about it?' asked Star.

'Look closer,' barked her brother. 'It's got a wire running from it.'

Star checked out the flagpole, the Stars and Stripes billowing in the wind. It was the highest point for miles around. She followwed the wire to a telegraph pole way below. 'It's probably the phone line,' she woofed.

'And our only chance of escape,' replied Spud, looking at the door in alarm. The stone had shifted. The guard dogs were just a few seconds away from a breakthrough.

Spud took off his helmet. 'Desperate times call for desperate measures,' he barked. Star watched as her brother clipped the strap on to the wire, his helmet hanging upside down. 'I've seen it on a film,' he yapped. 'It's called a zip wire. And there's one in the playground near our house.'

Star remembered. 'But that isn't a hundred metres up,' she barked. 'It's too dangerous.'

'No, *that's* too dangerous,' woofed Spud pointing to the door wedge, almost pushed out of the way. 'We've only got seconds to decide.'

Star looked at the door. The Rottweilers were throwing their bodies at it. She glanced at her brother, about to go on the ride of a lifetime. He was sitting in his helmet with one paw holding on to the ledge.

Certain death, she calculated as the door almost crashed down. *Or almost certain death*, she thought, imagining the scary zip-wire ride down to the telegraph pole.

Star put her paw to the clasp and undid her helmet. She jumped up to the flagpole just as the door splintered and the guard dogs fell into the top tower.

'Hi, guys,' waved Spud.

Star's paws were trembling as she tried to clip her helmet to the wire. The Rottweilers were all muscle but their snarling was even scarier.

Star panicked and lost her grip on her helmet. *Whoops*, she thought as the hat fell to the rocks below.

'Gotcha now,' snarled the biggest dog, venturing forward. 'Trespassing in our castle.'

'Come on, sis,' urged Spud. 'We'll have to share.'

The Rottweilers leapt towards the flagpole as Spud let go. He grabbed his

sister by the collar as he swooped by.

'Geronimoooo!' he yelled as the puppies hurtled downwards on the zip wire. 'Check out the view,' he woofed from the side of his mouth, his sister dangling dangerously over the side.

The helmet zinged along the wire, Spud squinting into the wind. 'It's a bit fast,' yelled Star, watching the telegraph pole approach. 'In fact, *very* fast,' she yelped. 'It's going to hur—' she barked as the helmet hit the pole and threw the dogs into the air. Thankfully, their fall was cushioned by a big bush.

Spud was first to his feet, wagging excitedly. He pulled his sister upright as she gasped for breath.

'You OK, sis?' he woofed, giving her a loving lick.

Star took a deep breath. 'Nothing broken,' she nodded, checking herself over.

'That was cool,' yelped her brother. 'Shall we do it again?'

16. SPELLING IT OUT

Ben, Sophie, Ollie and Lara wandered out of the Smugglers' Cafe. 'You see,' explained Ben, 'if it used to be where the pirates and smugglers hung out and it was called the "Castle Inn", maybe the legend of the castle gold is here. Not there,' he added, pointing up towards the stone building.

'After all,' chipped in Sophie, 'loads of people have searched Lord Whatsit's. But I bet nobody's ever searched the Castle Inn.'

Lara was listening intently. *You might have something*, she thought. *It's certainly an interesting idea. It'd be great if that horrible American guy had bought the wrong castle*, she smiled. Lara checked out the town hall clock. 'Best get back to the pups,' she woofed, stabbing her paw in the direction of Aunt Aggie's. *They will be nicely rested by now.*

'Looks like Lara wants to go and check on Star and Spud,' guessed Sophie. 'She's probably worried that they're up to no good!'

'No need to worry,' said Ollie matter-of-factly. 'There they are.'

Ben, Sophie and Lara turned to follow Ollie's finger.

Lara stood on her hind legs and rubbed her eyes. *No need to worry!* she gulped. *My puppies! What are they doing at the top of that tower?*

Ben squinted towards the castle. He could clearly make out two puppies up by the flagpole. 'How on earth did they get up there?' wailed Ben. 'I thought we told them no mischief?'

Lara was gone, bounding towards the castle at spy-dog speed. She watched in horror as her puppies slid down the wire, and arrived on the scene as Spud and Star staggered out from the bush.

'You certainly will *not* do it again!' woofed Lara in her most serious voice. 'What in heaven's name do you think you're playing at?' she panted, her chest heaving after the sprint. 'And *how* did you get into the castle?'

Spud and Star put on their sad faces—tails and bottom lips hanging low. 'Sorry,

111

Ma,' said Star, 'but there were some baddie dogs about to get us.'

'And we've been doing some spying,' blurted Spud. 'We followed a tunnel from inside Ollie's wardrobe. And it took us right into the castle.'

'And the man who owns it is digging for gold,' wagged Star, picking up the story. 'But he thinks it's at Aunt Aggie's so he's going round there, right now.'

'And he's got a gun—' panted Spud.

'Whoa!' woofed Lara. 'Slow down a bit,' she hushed, waving her paws to calm the puppies.

By the time the children caught up, Lara knew the whole story. She was still angry with them but that could wait for now. *If what they say is true, Aunt Aggie is in big trouble.*

Star bounded off and quickly came back carrying the helmet she'd dropped. 'The prof won't want both of these getting into the wrong hands,' she yapped, as Ollie took it from her.

Spud looked up at his helmet swinging from the wire above. 'Maybe it will make a good bird's nest?' he suggested.

Lara led the children down the rocky

path to the beach. *I have to communicate what's going on.* She took a stick and wandered over to a smooth bit of sand. *OK*, she thought, *here goes.* Lara fixed the stick firmly in her mouth and traced out a letter 'A'. *Oh, this is so slow*, she thought.

'Lara's doing a spy-dog thing,' grinned Ollie. 'She's spelling something for us. That's an "A",' said Ollie. 'For apple.'

Very clever, Ollie, thought Lara. *But this 'A' is for Aggie!* Lara continued with her message. The children watched as she added a 'G' and a 'Y'.

'"AGY",' said Ben aloud. 'What's "AGY"?'

'Aggie!' woofed Lara. *In text language. I haven't got all day to write her name out. There's a man with a gun visiting your aunt. Right now!*

'Spell "danger",' suggested Star. 'Then they'll get it.'

Lara went one better. She wrote 'GUN' in big letters.

'"AGY GUN",' said Sophie, shaking her head.

Yes, Aggie is being visited by a man with a gun! nodded Lara enthusiastically. *Got it?*

113

How about this? Lara took the stick and spelt out the letters 'GOL . . .'

'"Gold"!' yelled Ollie as Lara completed the 'D'.

Lara went back to 'AGY' and squeezed a little 'g' after the big one.

'"AGgY GUN GOLD",' read Sophie, looking horrified. 'Is it to do with Aunt Aggie and a gun?'

'Bingo!' woofed Lara, pointing excitedly at the little girl.

'Have the pups found the gold?' asked Ollie excitedly.

Not exactly, thought Lara. *But the men think it's at Smugglers' Cottage. If only you could understand me, kids.*

'Let's just ring the police,' said Ben firmly. 'Whatever's going on, they will sort it.'

'No way,' yapped the puppies, tearing round Ben's ankles like wild dogs. 'The policeman is a baddie!'

'Get away, pups,' said Ben, opening his mobile and punching 999. 'I'll make this call and then we'll get to Aunt Aggie's and tell her what's happening.'

'No!' barked Star. 'No police! Spud,' she woofed. 'Action stations.'

'Gotcha, sis,' he woofed. Spud went in front of Ben and crouched down. Star ran off and then came scampering towards her brother as fast as her stumpy legs would carry her. She sprang over him, leapfrog style and hurtled towards Ben. The boy had the mobile snatched from his ear just as the operator was asking 'Which emergency service?'

'Hey!' yelled Ben, chasing after Star. 'That's my mobile. Give it back!'

No chance, thought Star, sprinting for all she was worth. *If we ring the police that evil PC Winkle will get involved and he'll know we've worked out their plot.*

Ben gave up the chase. He watched in amazement as Star carried the mobile to the seashore. She waded into the icy water and flung her head sideways, hurling the phone into the frothy waves. 'There,' she barked. 'No police!'

Ben stood with his hands on his hips. He shook his head in anger and bewilderment and Star gave him a wide berth as she trotted out of the sea.

'I don't think they want us to phone the police,' guessed Sophie.

Don't worry, Ben, reassured Lara, wagging her tail and planting a lick on his hand. *We'll get you a new one. Let's go and check on Aunt Aggie.*

The group trudged back to Smugglers' Cottage, Ben glaring at Star and muttering with annoyance.

They got within fifty metres of the house and Lara put her paw out to stop the children. *Let me go first*, she warned. *I'll check it out. The pups said there was a man with a gun.*

Lara crept forward, the children tiptoeing behind. They all stood flat against the kitchen wall and listened. They could hear voices.

Shouting voices! Lara peered through the window and quickly shrank back to the children. *Not good*, she warned. *The men are there.*

'What's happening, Lara?' whispered Ben. 'Can I take a look?'

Be careful, nodded Lara.

Ben kept flat against the wall as he peered through the window, a look of horror making Sophie squeak with fear. He could see Aunt Aggie tied to a chair, with some parcel tape across her mouth. Her terrified eyes met Ben's and she quickly looked in another direction so as not to give him away.

'Aunt Aggie's tied up,' he whispered. 'Now we really need to phone the police. Except we can't.' He glared at Star.

I'm sorry, Ben, but that would make it worse, I promise, thought the puppy.

Ben ducked under the window and listened. 'The gold, lady,' he heard, in an American accent. 'It's not at the castle. And the tunnel leads here. So this is where it must be.'

Ben heard some banging and peered through the window again. PC Winkle was hitting the floor with a sledgehammer, shattering the kitchen tiles.

The American ripped the tape from Aunt Aggie's mouth. 'There's a chamber under here somewhere,' he yelled. 'If you tell us where it is, we won't have to smash up your house looking for it.'

Aggie shook her head. 'I don't know what you're talking about,' she said, her voice shaking with fear. 'And even if I did know, I certainly wouldn't tell *you*.'

Lord Burlington was also shaking. He

118

tore the sledgehammer from PC Winkle and attacked the floor with fury, sending splinters of tiles in all directions.

Ben crouched back down. 'They're after the gold,' he explained. 'They think it must be in the cottage. Aunt Aggie's being very brave,' whispered Ben, 'but we've got to figure out a way to save her.'

17. BREAKTHROUGH

Lara led the children and puppies to safety. *Even as a retired spy dog my priority is to do what's safest for the children*, she thought. *And my pups.*

Just then the heavens opened and they all took refuge in the bus shelter near the cottage.

Ben was anxious. 'I saw Aunt Aggie tied up,' he explained. 'And that policeman was smashing everything in sight. Looking for a tunnel, I think.'

All eyes fell on Lara. *I know, I know*, she thought. *We need a solution.* 'Star,' she woofed, 'and Spud. Good detective work to get us this far. Did Lord Burlington definitely have a gun?'

'Yes, Mum,' nodded Spud. 'An antique one. Like highwaymen used to use.'

Lara shuddered. *I've got to get the kids right away from the cottage and the gun.*

'What are we going to do, Ma?' asked Star. 'What's the spy-dog solution?'

Lara tugged at Ben's coat. *Follow me*, she woofed, dragging him across the road to the red phone box on the village green. *We need to ring the professor. He'll bring backup.* Lara stood on her hind legs and swung open the heavy door. Ben rummaged in his pocket and pulled out a coin.

'Who do you want me to call?' he asked. 'Mum and Dad?'

No way, thought Lara, shaking her head vigorously. She remembered how much trouble she'd been in in the past. Mrs Cook always blamed Lara for getting the children into dangerous situations. *And she can't come to the rescue with a broken leg anyway. No, Professor Cortex*, she woofed, taking her paw and writing 'CTX' in the condensation on the glass window.

'The prof,' said Ben excitedly. 'Of course!'

Got it in one, wagged Lara. *For once!*

Ben inserted the money and dialled the professor's mobile. 'Answer machine,' he mouthed to Lara before babbling, 'Hi, Professor, this is absolutely the most urgent thing ever. We're at Aunt Aggie's and she's been captured by some baddies who are looking for gold. It's a kind of accidental adventure, I promise. There're secret tunnels and stuff. And the local policeman is involved so we can't call the police. So Lara, I mean GM451, has made me phone you. Please help . . .'

Ben replaced the receiver and sighed heavily. 'My money ran out,' he said. 'With any luck, the prof will get the message and make his way here.'

And quickly, I hope! thought Lara.

Lara and Ben rejoined the others in the shelter and explained what they'd done.

Any other ideas, kids? Lara asked.

Spud rubbed his tummy. 'We could grab some food while we're thinking,' he suggested hopefully.

Lara frowned. 'Not now, lad,' she woofed. 'Your stomach is not my priority.'

'How about we explore this other castle,' suggested Ollie. 'Maybe we can find the treasure and then the baddies will let Aunt Aggie go? Or maybe there's another tunnel from there. The legend says there's a whole network of underground passageways. Nobody's ever searched the Castle Inn, I bet.'

Lara nodded. *And our special doggie noses may unearth something,* she hoped.

'And there's food in there,' wagged Spud before being cut down by another glare from his mum.

'Let's check it out,' woofed Lara. 'There's not much else we can do for now.' But there was one other option available to her. *I could leave the children and pups somewhere safe and I could take on the baddies. But they've got a gun,* she winced, thinking of her puppies and the hole in her ear, a souvenir of a previous adventure with a gun. *I am a black belt,* she thought. *But that doesn't make me a match for a bullet. I'll have to hope the prof gets here quickly to save Aunt Aggie.*

Lara led the gang to the Smugglers' Cafe.

'It's closed,' noted Ollie. 'Lights out. Door locked.'

But we have to get in, thought Lara. *This could be the key to the whole mystery. We won't be in real danger but if we can find the treasure maybe we can swap it for Aunt Aggie. Breaking and entering is nothing compared to the trouble she's in!*

123

*   *   *

Professor Cortex sank into his chair and reached for his cup of tea. He had sprinkled some home-made brain formula into it instead of sugar. He stirred and sniffed. 'Not good,' he admitted as the tea fizzed with blue steam. He always tested the experiments on himself first and would never feed anything to the animals that wasn't safe for humans. He was about to take a sip when he noticed the teaspoon had begun to melt. 'Mmm, perhaps not,' he murmured to himself. 'Need to reduce the strength a bit.'

The scientist reached for his mobile and noticed there was a missed call. He fumbled for his voicemail and placed the phone to his ear.

Ben's frantic voice came on the line. Professor Cortex dropped his cup of tea, ignoring it as it burnt a hole in the carpet. 'I don't believe it,' he grumbled. 'GM451 has got herself into another scrape!' He knew Mrs Cook was always quick to blame him, and although he failed to see how she could this time he was determined not to receive another telling-off. He heaved himself to his feet and checked the route on his satnav using the locator device inside Lara's collar. He tutted out loud. 'This is an emergency. Too far to drive.'

After all his years with the Secret Service Professor Cortex was still well connected. 'Time to call in a favour,' he explained to himself as his chubby fingers pressed the speed dial on his mobile. 'Agent A,' he barked. 'It's Maximus. I need a chopper. And I need it now.'

* * *

Lara instructed the children to wait while she and the pups disappeared round the back. 'Look for a way in, kids,' she instructed the puppies.

'Easy peasy,' noted Star. 'That window's open,' she woofed, pointing to the second floor.

'OK,' nodded Lara. 'But how do we get up there?'

'We don't,' woofed Star excitedly. 'I do,' she said, now pointing to the drainpipe. 'I can squeeze up the pipe to the roof and then swing myself in.'

Spud wagged excitedly. 'I can come too,' he woofed. 'And we can open a door or window and let you lot in.'

Lara and Star cast a glance at the drainpipe and then at Spud's waistline. They looked at one another and shook their heads. *The last thing I need is you stuck in a drainpipe*, she thought. 'You stay with me, fella,' assured Lara. 'Let Star carry out this part of the mission. You can help me later.'

Star scampered towards the black drainpipe and squeezed her body in. 'Perfect for puppies,' came the echoey bark. She used her paws to lever herself upwards. It was hard work but she made progress up the slippery, slimy pipe. The rain was dripping off the roof and down the drain, which meant there was a cold trickle of water running down her back. *And it's very scary*, she thought as she got higher.

Spud put his mouth to the base of the pipe and shouted, 'Are you there yet, sis?'

His bark boomed up the drainpipe and scared Star half to death. Her paws gave way and she almost fell, scrabbling for a hold. She righted herself and began to caterpillar her way upwards once more. 'I'm fine,' she yapped back to her brother. *This is so hard*, thought the tiny puppy. *My legs are aching.* The light at the top was getting closer. *Aunt Aggie's depending on me. My ma's a spy dog, best in the world. I want her to be proud of me!* She rested for a moment, her back against the pipe and hind legs stretched out to stop herself from falling. *I've got to go for it*, she decided, and off she went again, inching upwards.

After what seemed

127

an age, Lara and Spud saw a puppy's head popping out of the top of the drainpipe, like a chimney sweep's brush.

'She's there, Ma!' shouted Spud. 'She's made it.'

Star climbed out on to the roof and stood carefully, looking down at her brother and mum. She waved. *Hi, guys. Now to get through the window.*

'This looks like the hardest part, Star,' woofed Lara. 'Please be careful. I've wheeled this bin under you just in case. It's full of cardboard so it'll catch you if you fall.'

Falling wasn't in Star's vocabulary. She leant over the gutter and held on with her front paws and teeth. Her puppy body swung to and fro before she let go and disappeared into the window below. Lara and Spud heard a *thud* before a happy puppy face appeared at the window and gave the paws-up sign.

Lara and Spud raced round to the other side of the building as Star trotted down the stairs and appeared at the front window. She used her teeth and paws to loosen the catch. Ben helped pull the window open from the outside and they all climbed in. Lara was last through, looking around in case anyone had seen them breaking in. *We don't want some busybody upsetting our plan!*

The group huddled together in the Smugglers' Cafe.

'This is it, then,' announced Sophie. 'The original castle.'

'If we're right, the gold should be here,' said Ben. 'Let's find it!'

18. DOGGED DETERMINATION

Professor Cortex stood back as the helicopter landed nearby and the door popped open. He bowed his head as he ran towards it, his three strands of hair dancing in the wind. Slamming the door he gestured for the pilot to take off.

'No time to lose,' he yelled. 'We're going north. And quick!'

*   *   *

'It does feel a bit spooky,' said Sophie as they wandered through to the eating area. The cafe's empty dining room was dark and eerie. The suit of armour stood guarding the fireplace and the old portraits stared down at them. There were nets, ropes and an anchor hanging on the walls.

'Look at those pistols,' said Spud, pointing to the wall. 'They're just like the one the baddies have.'

'OK,' said Ben, 'we need to find clues.

But be quiet, everyone. We can't afford to get caught.'

The children tiptoed around the dining room. 'What are we looking for?' whispered Ollie.

'Not sure,' hissed Ben. 'Anything unusual, I guess.'

Star and Spud had their noses to the ground. Spud was straight over to the fireplace. 'Remember the smell of the wardrobe?' he woofed to Star. 'That kind of musty smell? Check this out,' he wagged, sniffing the hearth. Star joined him, tail upright.

'And there's a draught,' she barked, 'like there was in the wardrobe!' Spud stood in the fireplace and tapped his claw on the hearth. 'Hollow,' he said. 'Mum, I think we've found something.'

Lara bounded over. 'Good work, Spud,' she said, licking her son affectionately.

Ben wandered over. 'I think the pups have found something,' he said, poking about at the back of the fire. 'A draught,' he whispered. 'This is a false back. I bet there's a tunnel behind it.'

The pups wagged proudly. Ollie and

Sophie's eyes were shining as they all crowded around.

'What about ghost pirates?' asked Ollie.

'No such thing,' said Ben confidently. 'It's just a scare story to put people off finding the treasure.' He looked round at Lara. 'I'm going to have to smash a hole,' he said. 'It'll be noisy.'

'You can't just smash up someone's cafe!' protested Sophie, looking at her dog to back her up.

Lara thought for a second and nodded. *Go ahead, Ben. Aunt Aggie is in grave danger. We have to find the treasure. The owners have gone for the day*, she thought. *So let's go for it.*

Ben reached for the suit of armour and removed the axe from its grip. 'Sorry, old soldier, but I need to borrow this.' He took a firm hold with both hands and prepared to swing at the fireplace. 'Get back, everyone,' he warned, and they all took a step away. Ben swung the axe and it hit the tiles, sending splinters across the room. He swung again, this time with more confidence and the axe got wedged in a small hole. Ben pumped the handle up and down to release it. 'One more shot,' he said, swinging with all his might. The axe shattered its way through the back of the fireplace, revealing a dark hole. He shuffled forward to peer into the blackness.

'Any volunteers?' Ben asked. 'I won't fit through there.'

Ollie and Sophie took a step backwards. 'Too dark,' said Sophie.

'Ghost pirates,' reminded Ollie.

'Hidden treasure!' woofed Spud, stepping boldly forward. 'Agent Spud at your service.'

'And saving Aunt Aggie,' woofed Star.

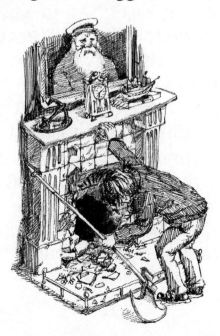

'Agent Star volunteering for action. We can squeeze through, Ma,' wagged Star. 'Let us follow the tunnel and see what we can find.'

Lara weighed up the options before giving them the nod. 'OK, pups,' she said. 'We'll stay here and keep looking while you check it out. I'll also keep an eye open for the professor. Hopefully, he'll be here in a little while and he'll have some backup. But don't do anything silly,' she added, thinking back to the zip wire. 'Just see what you can find out.'

Ollie handed over the helmet that Star had retrieved earlier. 'Here,' he grinned. 'You might want this to light the way.'

The helmet was fitted to Spud's head and immediately started capturing the energy from his tail, which was wagging rapidly with excitement.

'Careful,' warned Sophie, 'you'll blow the bulb with your enthusiasm!'

The puppies squeezed their way through the hole at the back of the fireplace.

'Take care,' woofed Lara, poking her nose after them. 'And, remember, don't get into any trouble!'

19. ATTRACTING ATTENTION

Spud led the way, the torch picking out cobwebs and one or two rats scurrying past.

'It's just like the passage behind the wardrobe,' woofed his sister, checking out the red-bricked walls. 'Same smell and everything.'

The pups tiptoed down some carved steps until the passageway levelled out. 'We're probably underneath the village green now,' woofed Star, judging the general direction. 'Heading to Aunt Aggie's!'

It was a long, straight tunnel, quite low in places. *Just about big enough for a small man*, thought Spud.

They came to a pile of earth where the roof had collapsed.

'Look!' complained Spud as the torch lit up the tunnel. 'It's blocking the way.'

'Well, let's do what we're good at,' suggested Star as she climbed up the pile of rubble and started digging.

The pups worked frantically to get

round the obstruction. Star finally made a hole near the top. They squeezed their way through and kept trotting.

'Another dead end ahead,' barked Spud, his lamp picking out a wall. 'But this one's solid.'

Star approached the wall and cocked her head, listening intently. 'Men,' she woofed. 'And a lot of banging.' Spud joined his sister and his floppy ears stood to attention.

It was muffled but they could make out the words. 'It's got to be here somewhere,' they heard Lord Burlington bellowing. 'Either the gold or the entrance to the smugglers' real tunnel.'

The pups looked at each other in alarm.

'I'll count to five, lady. I've given you enough chances. If you don't give me an answer this time, then you will be in very big trouble.'

Star scraped at the wall. 'The lord's got a gun,' she reminded her brother. 'We have to rescue Aunt Aggie.'

'One!' boomed the American.

Star's frightened eyes glowed in the torchlight. *What are we going to do?*

136

'Two!'

'Mum told us not to get into trouble but we have to help,' said Spud.

He began to bark and Star joined in. 'Leave her alone, you bully,' they woofed from behind the bricked-up tunnel.

'Three!' yelled Lord Burlington.

Spud imagined he was probably pointing the pistol at Aunt Aggie, her eyes filled with fear. The puppy used the metal part of the torch to bang on the tunnel wall. 'Pick on someone your own size!'

'Four!' screeched the man. 'I mean it, lady. Five's your limit.'

Spud banged louder, the sound echoing through the tunnel. Star barked her fiercest bark, her claws tearing frantically at the bricks.

'What's that?' they heard PC Winkle ask. 'Tapping and barking. From over there. Tapping in the fireplace.'

The puppies looked at each other and barked louder. 'Here, you bully,' woofed Spud. 'Come into this tunnel. Follow us to the real castle. You'll have my mum to answer to.'

Without warning the dogs heard an

almighty crash and a hole appeared in the wall right next to Spud's head. The policeman's huge nose peered through into the darkness. Spud took his opportunity and grabbed it with his

razor-sharp teeth. The man let out a blood-curdling scream but Spud held on. *I could get a taste for baddie blood!* He remembered a story his mum had once told him, about how she'd sunk her teeth into a baddie and held on. *So this is what I'm going to do too*, he thought.

An arm came through the hole and hit the puppy hard. *Ouch!* Followed by a frantic punch. Spud let go. There was another crash as the sledgehammer hit the bricks again. A bigger hole appeared and the puppies backed off a bit, snarling and yapping in fury. A boot kicked at the hole, widening it.

'What's going on in there?' shouted Lord Burlington.

'It's a rat or something,' replied PC Winkle. 'Bit me on the nose.'

'Rats don't bark, stupid,' said the American. 'It's dogs. Probably those puppies from earlier. Must be a tunnel. This could be it!' A hand came into the passageway and the puppies caught sight of a pistol waving in the light of their torch. 'I'll scare them off.'

Star ducked. Spud was on full guard-dog alert, his ears sticking up like yacht sails. There was a blinding flash of light and a noise so loud it sent the puppies tumbling to the ground. The lord withdrew his hand and reloaded his pistol. 'There,' he said, 'that should frighten the critters.'

He was right. Star and Spud turned tail and ran for their lives. They scampered along the tunnel in total darkness, Spud's tail between his legs. He forced himself to start wagging it again so they could see as the landslide approached. Once they'd squeezed past they finally stopped for a rest, their chests heaving.

'That was close,' gasped Star. 'Are you OK, bro?'

'Think so,' said Spud. 'But my ears are ringing. Must have been the noise of that pistol.'

The dogs scurried back to the Smugglers' Cafe and emerged through the hole in the fireplace.

'They're back,' yelled Sophie, picking up Star and giving her a hug.

'But what's happened to Spud?' yelled Ben. 'He's got a hole in his ear.'

'Have I?' said the puppy, putting his paw up to feel. 'Like Mum's?'

Lara hugged her son close. 'Who did this?' she asked. 'What on earth happened down there? I told you to be careful!'

'We heard the baddies threatening Aunt Aggie,' woofed Star. 'And we tried to distract them.'

'And they came after us,' barked Spud, 'but with a gun,' he continued, pointing at his holey ear.

'I think they're going to follow us down the tunnel,' warned Star.

Lara growled in frustration. *This is worse than I thought.* 'One thing's for sure,' she snarled. 'Whoever emerges from that tunnel is in for the fright of their lives!'

* * *

The policeman reloaded his pistol. 'That'll have scared them off,' he said, smiling at the smoking gun. Aunt Aggie winced in pain as the ropes round her wrists were tightened.

'It's no use struggling,' said Lord Burlington. 'You've seen what happens when I get annoyed,' he sneered.

As Aunt Aggie looked on, the two men smashed a hole large enough to scramble through and set off to explore the passageway. Each had a torch, and they strode purposefully, driven by the desire for gold. They soon arrived at the landslide.

'Go back and get a shovel quickly,' snapped the lord.

PC Winkle returned to the cottage for a shovel and Aunt Aggie glared at him as he disappeared back down the tunnel. All the while she hoped the puppies were going to appear from a snooze on one of the children's beds and save her. *I hope that barking wasn't them . . . or Lara*, she worried.

Back in the tunnel Lord Burlington and PC Winkle spent an hour clearing a way through the landslide. Muddied and sweaty, they scrambled through and set out towards the cafe. If someone else had found the treasure before them, there was going to be a showdown!

20. BOOBY-TRAPPED

'Ouch, it stings,' complained Spud as Sophie bathed his ear in the cafe's bathroom.

'It will hurt, silly dog,' tutted the little girl. 'You've been shot!' Sophie bandaged her puppy's ear and Spud bounded back into the thick of the action.

Lara instructed the puppies to set traps for the baddies. She'd calculated that the next people through that hole would be Lord Burlington and PC Winkle. *If they have a gun then we'd better booby-trap the place and get the kids out of the way.*

The children joined in with making traps. Ben had raided the kitchen. He'd poured cooking oil on the tiles by the fireplace. Sophie and Ollie had taken the ropes off the walls and tied them to the chairs as tripwires. 'Saw it on a film once,' grinned Ollie.

Spud had searched the kitchen for extra ammunition. *All I can find is mashed potato!*

Star, remembering her success with the window-cleaning burglar, had taken the gobstoppers from the shop and scattered them on the stairs.

Lara had been busy with a pan of soup. She'd also removed the sword from the display and left it resting on the cooker. Then she switched the cooker on to full and the electric hotplate began to glow. 'Keep clear of this,' she barked. 'Very hot!'

Lara managed to get Ben's help in tying a side of beef from one of the ropes. He heaved it to the side of the room so it was ready to swing. 'Let go of this rope,' he explained, 'and *wallop*! The baddies will be hit by half a cow.'

'All set?' asked Sophie.

All set, wagged Lara and her spy pups. Ben complained as the family pet shooed the children safely upstairs. *Sorry, guys, but this is a doggie mission.*

Lara jumped on to a chair and up to the window sill, hiding behind the curtain. 'Shush,' she hissed, paw to her lips. 'Any minute now.'

The puppies positioned themselves and lay in wait.

Spud was the first to hear voices. His bullet-holed ear was numb but in perfect working order. 'They're coming,' he woofed excitedly. 'Let's take them out.'

*　　*　　*

Professor Cortex's helicopter came in to land as he pointed to a field below. 'Set me down there,' he shouted. 'That's the car.' The helicopter landed and the professor made a stooped dash across the field. He jumped into the four-wheel drive Jeep and pulled down the sun visor, as he'd agreed with Agent A. The keys fell into his lap and he was away.

Within minutes he was driving through the village, heading for Smugglers' Cottage. He sped past the cafe and hit his foot on the brake. The tyres screeched and the professor jumped out. He ran to the cafe window where GM451 was sitting. The scientist tapped loudly and Lara nearly fell off the shelf in fright.

'GM451,' he yelled. 'What are you doing in there? Let me in, please. The children's aunt is in danger. I thought you were in charge? You've not got time to sit in a cafe having your tea!'

Lara sighed in frustration. *Go away, Prof*, she willed, urging him away with her paws. *Baddies are coming through the fireplace tunnel. Any second now!*

The professor marched to the front door and banged loudly. 'Let me in,' he ordered. 'What's going on in there, GM451?'

We're catching baddies, she thought. *I'll let you in later.*

Lara peered round the curtain just as the policeman's head appeared at the fireplace. *Yikes*, she thought, *that's a lot of blood!* She watched as he emerged from the hole and dusted himself down. Lord Burlington squeezed through behind him. He offered his colleague a hanky and he dabbed at the bloody nose.

'Gee, that's quite a scratch,' commented the lord.

'It's a bite,' PC Winkle reminded him. 'A vicious brute of a dog that, if I catch it, will be a dead dog.'

Spud gulped.

Lord Burlington pulled the pistol from his jacket pocket. 'Just in case,' he said, tapping it reassuringly. 'Where are we exactly?'

'The cafe, I reckon,' guessed the policeman, looking around at the tables. 'Nobody around, though—it's closed. Let's explore,' he said, taking a step forward.

'Now!' barked Lara. Star hit the light switch, plunging the cafe into darkness.

PC Winkle's boot hit the tiles and he slipped on the oil, his feet disappearing from under him in a comedy fall. His head hit the tiles with a crack. Lord Burlington was next, running on the spot before collapsing in a pile on top of his accomplice. His gun fell to the floor with a clatter. The pups came out of hiding and circled the men, yapping furiously.

Lara raced past and took up a new position behind the kitchen door.

The two men were dazed, and PC Winkle had a huge lump on his forehead. They clambered to their feet, holding on to each other like beginner ice skaters. PC Winkle hit the light switch and the puppies came into view.

'Puppies!' he yelled. 'One of you terrors bit my nose. You'll pay for that,' he roared. He grabbed the pistol and aimed it at Spud.

Yikes, thought the puppy, *I've already got a hole like Mum's. Don't want any more!* He and Star ran for it. Too late.

The gun went off with an almighty *bang.*

Missed! yapped Spud with relief.

The puppies kept running. Lara peered from the door, a smirk on her doggie lips. The policeman's face was covered with soot and his eyebrows went wild as he tried to wipe the black dust from his eyes. She'd switched his weapon

with one of the pistols from the wall of the cafe while the men were scrabbling on the floor. *I've loaded it with soot from the fireplace. So the gun is harmless, unless you're the one shooting it and then you get a face full of grime. Hopefully, he's learnt his lesson.*

Lara poked her head back to safety and ushered the pups silently into the kitchen. *Phase two.*

The baddies were aware of the booby traps and were being more careful.

'Come out here, you pesky mutts,' snarled the lord.

Lara heard a door open. Then footsteps. *I have to time this right*, she thought. And she did. A man came through the door and she brought the frying pan down hard on his head. Very hard. *Take that!* she thought at the satisfying *clunk* of metal on bone. Lara looked in horror as Professor Cortex slumped to the floor. *Whoops*, she thought. *That wasn't supposed to happen!* She dragged the unconscious professor out of the way and propped him up by the sink. 'Star, Spud,' she woofed. 'Throw some water on him.

Wake him up if you can.' Star did as she was instructed. Spud got busy sniffing for crumbs. This was a kitchen and he hadn't eaten for nearly two hours!

Lara was running out of strategies. She crept back to the door and put the finishing touches to her plan. She eyed the sword, still resting on the cooker. *Excellent*, she noted, *nice and hot*. 'This way, guys,' she barked.

PC Winkle shoved open the kitchen door and pointed at Spud, cowering in the corner. 'There you are!' he bellowed as the saucepan of soup fell from the top of the door. He was drenched in pea and ham gunge. The policeman wiped his face and advanced, angrier than ever. Star was pelting him with mashed potato. He spied the metal sword, placed temptingly on the cooker. *Go on*, urged Lara, *it's just what you need.*

PC Winkle reached for the handle and grabbed it, the sizzling sound of burning flesh drowned out by his scream. As he knelt down, yelling at his blistered hand, Lara had him right where she wanted him. She signalled to Spud, who opened the cellar door and pushed the man forward with all her might. Spud slammed it shut and they heard the policeman tumbling down the stairs. Lara secured the lock.

He's going nowhere, she thought. *One down, one to go!*

Professor Cortex opened his eyes and looked at the mess around him. 'What the dickens?' he began, shakily getting to his feet. 'GM451, what is going on?'

'Keep out of the way, Prof,' said Lara with a warning bark. 'There's still a baddie on the loose. Puppies, positions, please.'

'Winkle!' came a shout. 'Have you got rid of those dogs?' Lord Burlington barged through the kitchen door and Star let go of the rope, releasing the side of beef. It swung from the ceiling and missed the American by a fraction. Instead, Professor Cortex took the full force of the swinging cow and he slumped back to sleep.

Lord Burlington headed for the stairs. He got two steps up before he slipped a little but kept going. His momentum took him halfway up before Star's gobstoppers defeated him.

'Argh!' The lord bumped to the bottom of the stairs, hitting a different part of his body on each one.

Lara winced as he thudded down. *Ouch, ow, eek, aah, bump*, she thought as the man came to a stop at her feet. *That's gonna hurt.*

He looked around at the puppies and Lara. His head was spinning. 'Meddling dogs,' he declared, before Spud clonked him with a ladle and he passed out.

21. A LUCKY BREAK

The professor still looked a bit groggy a few days later. His bandaged head was thumping and both his eyes had gone black.

Everyone was enjoying a celebratory meal at the Smugglers' Cafe. Mr and Mrs Cook had driven up to collect the children as soon as they got the call.

'Poor Professor,' cooed Mum, her broken leg propped up on a chair. 'It must have come as a bit of a surprise.'

'That's an understatement, Mrs Cook,' he sniffed. 'Being clonked on the head by the spy dog I trained.' He glared at Lara. 'And then knocked unconscious by a large piece of meat. Most careless of you, GM451.'

I've said sorry, Prof, wagged Lara, planting a lick on his cheek. *You're my favourite scientist in the whole world. I didn't know it was you. I was protecting my pups and the kids.*

'So what happened after you'd got Lord Burlington and the policeman under control?' asked Dad.

'Lara, Ben and Sophie wrapped them up in clingfilm,' laughed Ollie.

'It's the only thing we could find in the kitchen,' explained Sophie. 'Quite effective. They were trussed up so tightly they couldn't move.'

'By the time the real police arrived they were all sweaty,' grinned Ollie. 'And very angry!'

'I bet,' agreed Mum. 'But I'm glad to hear that you all helped the cafe owners clear up and get the place back to normal. And how are you feeling now, Aggie? It must have been awful to have been tied up and threatened like that.'

Aggie nodded but her positive attitude remained. 'These brilliant children saved me,' she said, beaming at Ben, Sophie and Ollie. 'And the dogs,' she added, waving her hand around the room at Lara and the pups.

Star and Spud sat proudly at the table. *Our first adventure*, wagged Spud. *We bagged a couple of baddies and saved Aunt Aggie. Not bad for trainee spies.*

A waiter cleared their plates and disappeared back to the kitchen.

'It seems the power cuts were deliberate,' said Aunt Aggie. 'The men had been cutting the wires, trying to scare me. And all that banging in the night had been them clearing the tunnel. Then that awful American kept offering to buy the house. I guess he thought that I'd get fed up and sell.'

'A shame you didn't unearth the treasure, though,' commented Dad, munching on some crusty bread.

'A real shame,' agreed the waiter, returning with some cheesecake and plonking it in front of Mum. 'I was kind of hoping you might have found it here. I mean, this was the "Castle Inn", after all.'

'Probably melted down,' said the professor. 'And spirited away. Years ago, I shouldn't wonder.'

'What's going to happen to the real castle?' asked Ben. 'Now that His Lordship and the policeman are in jail.'

'Not sure,' replied Aggie. 'I guess it'll just be left to ruin. Which is a real shame because if it had some money spent on it we'd make it into a brilliant tourist attraction.'

'Mum,' barked Spud. 'I've finished my cheesecake. May I leave the table, please?'

Lara nodded. 'Take your napkin out of your collar,' she said.

'And me?' asked Star, holding her paw up, asking for permission.

'Off you go, the pair of you,' she said. 'But *no* mischief.'

Star and Spud sniffed for interesting smells. The floor smelt of cooking oil. 'It's been cleaned but it's still a bit slippery,' said Star, taking a run up and gliding across the floor.

'Hey, that looks cool,' woofed Spud, galloping to the other end of the room to take a run-up.

'Careful,' warned Lara. 'Don't overdo it.'

Spud wasn't listening. He scampered towards the fireplace, hit the oil slick and slid on his furry bottom. 'Yippee!' he squealed as he sailed past everyone.

'Careful!' warned Lara. 'Watch out for the armour.'

Spud looked up at the suit of armour. It was getting closer. And fast! He had no brakes. The puppy sailed headlong

into the metal suit, crunching into its shins.

'Out of the way, everyone!' shouted the professor as the armour creaked, toppled and fell. The two-hundred-year-old outfit crashed to the floor and everyone stared in open-mouthed silence.

Er, sorry, wagged Spud. *I had a bit of an accident. Again!*

The helmet rolled across the floor and

lay at Ben's feet. He picked it up and everyone's eyes were drawn to a glint of gold.

'That's pretty,' said Sophie.

Professor Cortex reached for the helmet and banged it on the tiled floor. He chipped away some of the coating and more sparkly gold was revealed. 'And feel the weight,' he said, passing it to Dad.

'Gosh,' said Dad, taking the heavy helmet. 'There's only one metal that weighs this much.'

'It's an alloy, actually,' corrected the scientist. 'Usually mixed with silver and platinum. Sometimes with copper too.'

'Gold!' exclaimed Ben.

'Exactly,' said the professor, chipping more of the coating away. 'I think the suit of armour is made of solid gold. Just covered over with grey paint to hide it.'

'Wow!' said Ollie, his eyes wide with excitement.

'So the treasure's been in *this* castle for centuries. Melted down and made into a suit of armour!' said Sophie.

'Under everyone's noses,' exclaimed Aggie.

Brilliant, thought Lara.

'We've solved the puzzle,' barked Star.

'And I found the hidden treasure,' yapped her very proud brother. 'Maybe I'll qualify as a spy pup after all!'

22. REPORTING FOR DUTY

Lara held the newspaper up to the puppies. 'Check it out,' she woofed. 'We've made the news!'

'"Gold Diggers",' read Spud, his eyes shining with excitement.

Star was the best reader so she scanned the article and barked it to her brother. '"A two-hundred-year-old mystery was solved and two criminals arrested for their part in a daring robbery. American citizen Arthur Burlington and his accomplice, PC Frederick Winkle, are expected to receive long sentences for armed robbery."'

'Quite right too,' wagged Spud. 'What else does it say?'

'"A local restaurant owner has unearthed a golden suit of armour. The legend of the castle gold was solved when tourists accidentally knocked over the armour, revealing it to be made of *solid gold*." And here's a picture of Aunt Aggie. Check out her grin,' said Star, slapping the paper with her paw. 'And

look at her quote. 'She says "Mr
Burlington is swapping gold bars for
prison bars." Nice one, Aunt Aggie.'

'Apparently he isn't even a proper lord,' explained the professor. 'He just called himself Lord Whatever because he owned the castle. Turns out he's got a long criminal record. He's wanted in America too.'

Spud's ears were on full alert, sunlight shining through the bullet hole. 'And what's the cafe owner doing with the money?' he woofed.

'It says the gold isn't his,' explained Star, her eyes following the story. 'The treasure is actually owned by the whole village. They're using the money to buy the castle and renovate it. It says they're going to make it into a wonderful tourist attraction,' she read. 'Just what Aunt Aggie wanted.'

Lara breathed a sigh of relief. *It's been a frantic few weeks! And a relaxing stay at Aunt Aggie's has turned out to be anything but relaxing. Maybe things will quieten down from now on and we can get back to normal family life.*

'No mention of us, though,' said Star, her tail drooping slightly.

'That's because we're following in our mum's footsteps,' yapped Spud, sitting up. 'Working on special missions,' he said, standing to attention and sucking his stomach in. 'Keeping our abilities secret.'

Lara winked at the professor and he stepped forward and cleared his throat. 'If I may have your attention for just a minute,' he said. All doggie eyes fell on the scientist. 'I have to admit,' he began, 'that I've been very impressed with your investigative work. Very impressed indeed.'

Lara glowed with pride. *They are rather special.*

'And I've had discussions with GM451 about code names,' added the professor.

Star and Spud sat up straight, controlling the urge to wag. *Code names, like proper spies! How thrilling!*

'GM451 isn't keen on numbers,' explained Professor Cortex. 'A bit too formal for her. So we've come to a compromise.'

The pups cocked their heads in concentration.

'Star,' added the professor, 'you are now "Special Tactics and Rescue".'

Spud could feel his sister's tail bashing

him in excitement.

'And you, young pup, are "Super Performing Undercover Dog".'

'Woo hoo!' Spud backflipped and scampered across to the professor for a hug. The old man grinned as he patted the dog's head. 'You two are the world's first ever "Spy Pups".'

'What do you think of that?' barked Lara.

'For real?' woofed Star.

'For real,' assured Lara.

'We're not just any old puppies,' howled Spud. 'We're Spy Pups. Code names STAR and SPUD, reporting for duty.'

The puppies put their paws to their eyebrows in a double doggie salute. 'And long may our adventures continue!'